Evelyne saw Gabriel's eyes ~~~~~~~~~~~~~~. She tried to recover, but it was too late. He'd seen.

He pointed at her—at her stomach. "What is that?" Gabriel demanded.

She had dreamed of this in her weaker moments. Telling him that he was to be a father. In her fantasies, she was calm, casual, disdainful almost. She did not give him the satisfaction of thinking that she needed him, wanted him, or was afraid of being alone.

She was determined to make fantasy a reality.

So she beamed at him, made sure she sounded cheerful. "In the States they call it a baby bump." She ran her hands over the roundness, moved to give him a profile view. Refused to let the nerves fluttering through her show—she'd had ample practice at hiding those. "Isn't that cute?"

He said nothing. Didn't move. She wasn't sure he breathed.

When he finally moved, it was with clear-cut precision. "Explain yourself," he said quietly, dangerously.

She chose to maintain her flippancy. "Is it not self-explanatory, Gabriel? I am pregnant."

A sensationally thrilling Harlequin Presents duet from Lorraine Hall.

Babies for Royal Brides

From wedding ring to royal heir!

The royal family of Alis live a fairy-tale existence. At least, they're *supposed* to. But whilst Crown Prince Alexandre and Princess Evelyne were born into a world of privilege, they grew up under their father's iron rule. Now they're planning to rip up the King's royal rule book! But could two marriages of convenience followed by two pregnancies not just rewrite the kingdom's future, but give Alexandre and Evelyne the chance to experience a love they thought only happened in storybooks?

You're cordially invited to the wedding of...

Evelyne and Gabriel
Secretly Pregnant Princess
Available now!

Ines and Alexandre
Coming soon...

SECRETLY PREGNANT PRINCESS

LORRAINE HALL

Harlequin

PRESENTS

MIX
Paper | Supporting responsible forestry
FSC® C021394
www.fsc.org

ISBN-13: 978-1-335-21350-1

Secretly Pregnant Princess

Copyright © 2026 by Lorraine Hall

Harlequin Enterprises ULC
22 Adelaide St. West, 41st Floor
Toronto, Ontario M5H 4E3, Canada
www.Harlequin.com

HarperCollins Publishers
Macken House, 39/40 Mayor Street Upper,
Dublin 1, D01 C9W8, Ireland
www.HarperCollins.com

Printed in Lithuania

Lorraine Hall is a part-time hermit and full-time writer. She was born with an old soul and her head in the clouds, which, it turns out, is the perfect combination to spend her days creating thunderous alpha heroes and the fierce, determined heroines who win their hearts. She lives in a potentially haunted house with her soulmate and rambunctious band of hermits-in-training. When she's not writing romance, she's reading it.

Books by Lorraine Hall

Harlequin Presents

The Forbidden Princess He Craves
Playing the Sicilian's Game of Revenge
A Diamond for His Defiant Cinderella
A Wedding Between Enemies
Pregnant, Stolen, Wed
Unwrapping His Forbidden Assistant

The Diamond Club

Italian's Stolen Wife

Rebel Princesses

His Hidden Royal Heirs
Princess Bride Swap

Work Wives to Billionaires' Wives

The Bride Wore Revenge

Visit the Author Profile page at Harlequin.com.

For the protectors.

CHAPTER ONE

Princess Evelyne Lucia Martina Lidia had been summoned to her father's office often in her almost twenty-four years. It was *never* a good thing.

Still, today, she was lighter than usual. Because tonight, her brother was to be married. And a royal wedding for the heir meant a respite for Evelyne. Whatever complaints her father levied against her this morning, whatever punishments for petty infractions about to be doled out, they were small prices to pay for a little bit of freedom.

It wouldn't last forever. No doubt Father would be back to scheming her into the marriage mart soon enough—but Alexandre's wedding, and hopefully a royal baby soon after, should take the heat off for at least a year.

Within a years' time, she could convince Jordi to either stand up to her father or run away with her. He loved her. Said so all the time. As a royal aide, she knew he had a deep fear of upsetting her father, and who could blame him? King Enzo was a volatile, violent, *evil* man.

But with enough time, Evelyne was sure…she was *sure* she could convince Jordi to be as brave as she was willing to be.

For love, she thought dreamily.

But all dreams died when walking into King Enzo's grand office. Luxurious, gleaming gold that always gave her a headache, and her father always dressed in some uniform or another. He'd never actually trained or served in the Alis military, but he liked to stomp around in his role as *leader* as though he had.

Mostly, it was to intimidate. Such was Enzo's way. No one loved or respected the king, his children included. He was a mean, petty man full of spite, hate, and obsessed with retribution. Evelyne did not remember her mother as she'd been told the queen died in childbirth, but Evelyne wouldn't have been surprised to find Enzo had killed her.

He was that horrible. And on those occasions he beat her—something she knew her brother did his level best to stop—she could see it in his eyes. The fact was he *would* kill, given the right opportunity. Evelyne would have run away long ago, but her father was powerful, and his little spies were scattered across their small country. He ruled with the iron fist of a dictator, and everyone fell into line. Even her.

For now, she told herself.

All who existed in their little country waited for the day that King Enzo would die, and Prince Alexandre would take the throne. There was no doubt in Evelyne's mind that Alexandre was the best man in the world, and everything would be all right once her brother was the king.

Whether it be true or not didn't matter. What mattered was hope.

But for this morning, as she walked into her father's office, she found her hope a little unsteady. Because yes, her father was there in his usual military uniform with his usual smug expression on his face, but Alexandre was here as well. He was not yet dressed for his wedding, nor did he wear an expression fit for a soon-to-be-groom. His mouth was in a grim line, his dark eyes flat.

She knew he did not love his fiancée. He was doing his duty. *That* was Alexandre. She might have hated him for being so good, so perfect, but in doing his duty, he often protected *her* from whatever plans their father had for her.

Still, she felt sorry for Ines, because it was unclear whether the soon-to-be-bride believed her marriage into the Lidia royal family was one based on money and power, or one based on love.

There was no love in this kingdom as long as Evelyne's father ruled.

Father glanced at the large watch on his wrist. "I summoned you ten minutes ago, child."

She didn't point out that the palace was huge, that it took *time* to get from one end of it to the other. She'd learned her lesson about arguing with him as a young girl.

Eventually.

"My apologies, sir." She gave a regal curtsey. Mostly for Alexandre's benefit. Because he was here and it was his wedding day, and she knew her father was just *itching* to punish her in some way to make Alexandre's day even more miserable.

Father eyed her, which would have been enough for the warning alarms in her head to sound, but then he eyed Alexandre, and smiled.

"On this happy day where Alexandre submits to his duty and marries, I would like to inform you that you will soon follow."

Evelyne did not allow herself to react outwardly. She

kept her expression placid and bland. She did not look Alexandre's way like she wanted to. She didn't even dare clasp her hands together or demand to know what he meant. She stood, settled into her regal bearing and waited for the bomb to drop.

"I have long sought the right man for you to marry, Evelyne. It has been quite the ordeal since you prefer to be so…rebellious."

Evelyne couldn't remember the last time she'd *rebelled* against him, unless he knew about Jordi. Which made her cold all the way through.

"He must be strong, of course. Powerful. Someone worthy of being the father of royal children, but someone who would not simply do whatever *you* told him to do." Father came around to rest a hip on his desk. He surveyed her with analyzing eyes. "Someone unafraid to use whatever methods might keep you in line."

Might. In line. This time Evelyne could not resist looking back at her brother. Who stood exactly as he had been, but his expression had moved far closer to fury than it had been.

"General Sergi Vinyes has expressed an interest in you, my dear."

If she thought she'd been cold before, now her blood was nothing but ice. She couldn't breathe. General Sergi Vinyes was a monster, as bad as her father if not worse. She knew she could not say that to her father, but she also couldn't hold her tongue completely.

"He's more than twice my age, Father." And known for his brutal tactics on the military fields—not with enemies, mind you. Because despite Enzo's blood lust, he had not engaged in a full-on war *yet*. The general was known for his cruelty with his *own men*.

"What of it? I was more than twice your mother's age when we married." He smiled as if this was a positive, something to brag about.

Evelyne wanted to retch.

"Father," Alex said in that calm, firm voice of his that allowed Evelyne to think there was some hope of getting out of this. "I am getting married tonight. And, with any luck, there will be a royal baby announced by next year. There is no need to rush Evelyne into marriage. She is young, and it is best to spread the pomp and circumstance out a bit, don't you think?"

"She will accept Sergi's proposal when it is offered. End of story."

He turned his back on both of them, a sign of dismissal. But Evelyne…

"I will not marry him." Could not. Would not. There was no arguing with her father, but she could not marry the violent general twice her age.

Very slowly, Father turned to look at her with that icy blue gaze of his. She felt Alexandre come to stand behind her, but she knew… Even two against one they would not win.

"You will," Father said very quietly. "It is not your decision to make."

Alexandre put his hand on her shoulder. "Evelyne, let this rest for now," he murmured in her ear.

"I will kill myself before I marry him." And she meant it. She would not suffer through that. It was bad enough the way her father treated her, the punishments she was subjected to. She would not be bartered off into even more violence.

"Ah, Evelyne." Father tsked. "You will not have the chance."

She saw it so clearly. She would not have the chance.

She thought she'd been about to experience some modicum of freedom, and instead she was sentenced—far earlier than expected—to an even worse jail than the one she'd imagined.

No. No, she wouldn't take it. She *wouldn't*. She turned on a heel and ran.

She ignored Alexandre calling her name. She had to find Jordi. He was her only hope. And she still had hope. They would run away together. He would take her away. France. Spain. The end of the *world*, she didn't care. Just away.

Since Jordi was one of Alexandre's aides, he was quite busy with wedding preparations. But that meant Evelyne knew exactly where to find him. With just hours before the wedding, he would be in the ceremony hall, dealing with last minute details.

She ran down hallways, upstairs, and when at last she found him in the ballroom double-checking seating assignments, she ran right to him, grabbed his arm. "Jordi."

"Evelyne, calm down." He gave her a scowl—she'd called it handsome on more than one occasion, perhaps perversely enjoying his occasional disapproval.

Because sometimes he did not approve or agree, but he *loved* her just the same. *Regardless*. She did not have to be anyone but herself with Jordi.

"Jordi," she repeated, breathless from running. "Father has insisted I accept a proposal from General Vinyes. We must run away! We'll run away together. It's the only way."

Jordi looked at her like she was speaking in tongues, but he patted her hand. "Calm down, Evelyne."

"Calm down? Are you listening to me? General Vinyes. I cannot marry him. We must leave the palace at once."

"Your brother's wedding…"

"That is why we must go now. Alexandre will understand. Come." She tugged on his arm, but he did not budge.

"Evelyne… I cannot go against your father. He is a *king*. Do you know what he'll do to me?"

"That's why we'll run away." Panic had big, heavy wings now, beating against her chest. Why wasn't he rushing to help her? Why wasn't he rushing to agree? Why was he looking down at her with something close to pity?

"Don't you understand?" she implored him. "He won't change his mind. We must…" It dawned on her then. "You were never going to marry me."

"Evelyne, come now."

Which was neither agreement nor rebuttal. Which made her realize that all the plans they'd made had been… hers. And he'd never disagreed with her, never told her she was fanciful or in the wrong.

But he never agreed. Never supported. Never *acted* to make any of her dreams come true.

Because he'd always known. She saw it so clearly now, in this terrible moment where her future was turning to darkness. *She'd* let herself build a fantasy on him. *He'd* let her.

But fantasy was all it was.

Fine enough to risk the king's wrath when he got a

princess sneaking into his bed out of the deal, but not enough to actually...*do* something.

"You said you loved me." That he *had* said.

And it was a lie.

"Let us not make a scene at your brother's wedding," Jordi said, patting the hand that held on to him. When the wedding wasn't set to start for another few hours.

She looked at him, his handsome face. Those green eyes she'd been so taken with that refused to meet her gaze. The way he held himself, leaning slightly back as if he was afraid she might transfer a sickness to him.

The sickness of being a Lidia.

Something inside her broke. Whatever youthful naïveté she'd managed to hold on to in this place. Whatever belief she'd had that Jordi might have seen her and loved her, was gone, and with it...all her hopes for a future out of her father's influence.

She heard her name, turned to see two of her father's guards striding toward her. Because she would not be given a moment of freedom any longer, not after threatening to kill herself. So now it was all over.

Hope was dead.

Gabriel Marti did not relish spending time in Alis. He found the small, military-obsessed country stifling. His father had been born here, had been a diplomat from Alis to Italy when Gabriel had been born, but had fallen in love in Italy. Though Gabriel had spent his very early years in Alis, his father had moved them to his mother's home country before King Enzo had gotten too obsessed with might and violence and canceled all diplomacy to other countries.

He'd gotten them out just in time too. Not long after Gabriel had turned eight, King Enzo had shut down the borders and kept all citizens prisoners, essentially. Father would often lament that Enzo was a simple man who had followed the simple adage—absolute power corrupts absolutely.

Gabriel would not visit at all, but Prince Alexandre Lidia had been his best friend since he could remember. First here at the palace, and then at the boarding school his parents had allowed him to attend so that he and Alex could continue their friendship.

Gabriel owed Alex much, his entire life, really. So he'd spent the past week at the Lidia palace preparing for the royal wedding where he would stand up for his friend.

Besides, Gabriel had long ago learned that finding *humor* in a complicated situation was far better than getting sour about it, taking it too seriously, and then traveling the path toward ruin.

Sometimes he worried that visits to Alis would end with the king finding some way to keep him here. One never knew with King Enzo, and since Gabriel had built himself up into an independent, wealthy businessman, he knew the king had *some* interest in him, claiming him to Alis in some way.

But so far, he had outwitted all the king's attempts to keep him here and claim him as an Alis citizen. Gabriel was confident in his skills…but not so arrogant to ever let his guard down.

This trip, the king had been surprisingly hands-off. Gabriel hoped it was because he was busy and wrapped up in the wedding, but he still didn't let his guard down.

All throughout the ceremony, and into the reception, he kept himself in a group at all times.

And since he valued enjoyment and having a good time no matter the circumstances, mostly the groups were made up of beautiful, glittering women.

Until Alexandre came up to him and handed him a glass of wine. The smile was fake. No matter how good Alexandre was at being stoic, Gabriel had known him long enough so that he knew how to read him. He also knew that if Alex was moving him toward a shadowy corner, away from the flirtatious royals, debutants, and so on, it was for good reason.

"I need you to do me a favor," Alex said, his voice low and intense. His gaze tracked around the room. Gabriel noted the king was currently talking to the bride and her parents. Occupied. But Alex kept his dark gaze on his father.

"On your wedding night? Shouldn't you be more concerned with your new bride?"

Alex's gaze moved to Ines. His expression seemed to grow more grim, if possible. Gabriel knew there was no great love match there. If anything, Alex and Ines tolerated each other for the greater good.

Gabriel thought it was a pity. He wasn't sure he believed in something as deep and abiding as soul mates. Such depth of feeling would be dangerous, no doubt. But he had spent his childhood in the warmth of his parents' good marriage and figured a bad one would be rather soul sucking.

Ines was a pretty thing, but…fragile seeming, and the huge white confection of a dress did little to dispel that aura. She seemed the kind of fragile that would never survive life in the Lidia palace.

Oh, Alexandre was a good man who would try to protect her, because nothing survived here without Alexandre's protection. But Gabriel had his doubts that even Alex could save Ines from the life she was about to lead.

"Evelyne," Alex said, mentioning his sister. "You must use one of your escape routes and take her away."

Gabriel choked a bit on the drink he'd taken. He coughed, cleared his throat. "Away?" he croaked.

"Without anyone knowing where. Including myself."

"Alex…" This was a great task. One with immense meaning. And great risk to Gabriel.

"My father has promised her to General Sergi Vinyes."

Gabriel looked across the ballroom to the woman in question. Evelyne had no aura of fragility like Ines. She was bright and vibrant, a shining beauty. He had often wondered how she maintained it in a place such as this, with a father such as hers.

Evelyne was another reason Gabriel did not care for spending time in Alis these days. As she'd grown into a beautiful young woman, she'd become a temptation. For some time, Gabriel had made certain to indulge *all* his temptations.

But Evelyne was one that reminded him of the adolescent he'd been—full of rage and obsession. Alex had saved him from that, so he could not go back to it. Certainly not because of his little sister.

Like every other sane person in this palace, he owed Alexandre too much to fool around with the prince's sister.

But no one deserved General Vinyes. Gabriel didn't

even know the man, spent very little time in Alis, and still the military man's reputation for blood lust, revenge, and fury was something well known across Europe. Something that kept many countries from invading this small, belligerent one.

So no, no one deserved the general. Certainly not a young, vibrant princess as beautiful as Evelyne.

Tonight she was dressed in a glittering green dress that didn't match the wedding colors but complemented them. The garment skimmed along her curves, a sensuous delight Gabriel knew better than to allow himself to notice. Her hair—somewhere between a honeyed blond and a shiny chestnut—was pulled back in an elaborate twist. Her lips were painted a dark, purplish red that would have short-circuited his brain if he allowed his vision to linger there.

Instead, he noted the two serious-looking guards who flanked her, both armed.

"Get her away from the guards without causing suspicion," Alex was saying fervently. "Get her out of here. Take her somewhere she won't be found. If possible, on a plane that can't be tracked to either of us. Tonight. Then set her up with a new life. While my father is distracted and thinks I've no time to plan. I will pay you back when I am able. It is too much to ask, I know this, but I must ask it anyway. She cannot be married to that monster."

In any other situation, Gabriel might have led with a joke, with the aura of casual nonchalance, but not with Alex. Not with the one man in the world he allowed himself to owe.

"There is no ask too big, Alex," he said, even knowing this *was* the biggest ask for a wide variety of reasons. "You once saved my life," Gabriel reminded him.

Alex sighed impatiently as he often did when Gabriel brought it up. If Alexandre had faults, his stark refusal to admit he was near saint levels of *good* was one of them.

Gabriel looked at Evelyne and the guards once more. He'd have no trouble getting her out of the palace—he and Alex had studied and planned escape routes for nearly two decades now. And thanks to that, Gabriel's entire personal fortune was built on understanding and implementing security for the well-connected wealthy, the royal.

And since it was, he knew how to get around it, especially since he'd designed and implemented much of the palace and country's security himself.

But the guards... They were under King Enzo's command and King Enzo's command alone. Getting around them would take some doing. Not that Gabriel had any doubts he could accomplish it, but it would require time with Evelyne. In that dress. "Have you told Evelyne of your plan?" he asked, his mind already imagining and rejecting ideas.

"No, I'm afraid she'll...do something unwise if I give her warning. You must simply whisk her away. You can tell her my plan once she's on a plane. Safe from the king."

They both looked at the king across the room, holding court. Gabriel was well acquainted with evil—the different shapes and sizes of it that existed within men. So often it came cloaked in power, influence. So often it hurt the glittering innocents like Evelyne. He had found that even power and money could not always protect a woman in this cruel world.

King Enzo knew how to wield it all. As General Vinyes would.

No, he could not allow such to be wielded against Evelyne, both for Alex and for the princess herself.

"I trust you, Gabriel. With my sister's safety."

And because Alexandre had once saved him from the evil he had been close to succumbing to those years ago, Gabriel nodded, now determined.

He would help Evelyne, regardless of personal sacrifice, and honor the debt he owed her brother.

And he would certainly keep his hands to himself while he did it.

CHAPTER TWO

EVELYNE WAS NOT much of a drinker, but tonight she set herself to the task. Hope was gone, why *not* make a scene? If her father punished her, so be it. Before today, she'd had some vague hope that *eventually* the king would die of bitterness and old age.

But now she had two captors lined up. Even with the general being more than twenty years older than her, hoping for *two* men's death in order to be free was too great a weight to hold.

What was the point of anything now?

Father and General Vinyes would keep her from even the escape of death. She had no doubt they could, based on how close two of her father's guards stayed to her throughout the afternoon, ceremony and now reception. So far, her only respite had been to use the restroom, and they'd been waiting for her right outside when she was done.

Any room with *windows*, they followed her into. Like she'd fling herself from one given the chance.

But the worst part was she didn't *want* to die. She simply didn't want to suffer anymore. Was that so wrong?

She downed her third glass of champagne, and since the guards didn't stop her from doing such, she went over to the bar to procure her fourth. She'd ask for something harder, but she was afraid they'd stop her. So she'd settle for drinking as much champagne on an empty stomach as humanly possible.

She could already feel a pleasant fizzing sensation in her mind, in her body. She felt a little unsteady and *liked* it.

It was the only thing she liked. The guards, she knew, were a hint of what was to come, and it made everything…horrible. Because while she'd spent some twenty years devising ways around her father's punishments— mental and physical—this seemed to be the last unsurmountable challenge to finding an even somewhat pleasant life amid her royal shackles.

"Good evening, Evelyne."

The voice was familiar, but she was surprised to find a hand on her elbow to go with it. Gabriel Marti *never* touched her. Her brother's best friend tended to avoid her. If he could not, he often treated her like an amusing but spoiled child.

It grated, and he knew it. She had no doubt that's why he did it. He was the kind of man who read a room and behaved accordingly. Sometimes she wanted to hate him.

But sometimes, she could admit, she wanted to throw herself at him. Handsome and competent, people *laughed* when they were with Gabriel. Gabriel himself smiled and charmed.

There was none of that in the palace when he wasn't around.

So she could admit surprise, and a flutter of interest, at his large hand on her elbow, a warm, steady strength and counterpoint to all the upheaval inside her.

Saying nothing else, he expertly navigated her away from the bar before she could get that next glass of champagne—smart move—and toward one of the terrace doors.

"It was a lovely wedding," he said, his voice low and pleasant in her ear.

"It was." She glanced over her shoulder to where Alexandre stood with his bride while they spoke to a couple Evelyne didn't recognize. "I hope they can be happy." Someone should be. Maybe Alexandre didn't love Ines, but if they could find some *solace* in each other, maybe…

Gabriel opened a terrace door, but before he ushered her out into the glittering evening, he smiled at the guards who had fallen into step behind them. "I will keep an eye on her for a bit, gentleman. The prince's orders." Then he led her outside.

Onto the terrace, but he didn't stop there. He kept pulling her along, down the grand staircase and into the gardens that were lit with fairy lights and candlelight and little bonfires so guests could enjoy the grounds despite the chill in the air.

"They're still following us," Evelyne pointed out. She would never be free. Never, ever, *ever*. Tears filled her eyes, but she refused to cry again. She'd had a nice jag over Jordi. Now…

Now what?

"Yes, but they've given us more space. There's a lot we can do with more space."

She glanced up at him. He didn't *deliver* it like innuendo, but she had to admit that's where her mind flitted.

The alcohol probably. And the fact he was outrageously handsome. So tall, his dark hair swept back in a careless kind of style that somehow felt both casual and perfectly suited for a royal wedding. His eyes were a kind of hazel, she supposed, a fascinating array of greens and browns with a hint of blue. His suit was dark, elegantly tailored, but simple when compared to Alexandre's royal costume for the wedding.

This close, she could smell expensive aftershave, champagne and the hint of something else, smoky almost. Intriguing.

And it was nice, to be intrigued, to notice all these things, rather than drown in her own misery.

Gabriel moved her through the maze of pathways, arm in arm, talking lightly of the weather, of Alex, of Ines. The guards kept their distance, one even peeled off and lit a cigarette. They must trust Gabriel to keep her in line or keep her from hurtling herself onto the nearest sharp object.

She considered if *she* trusted the charming, roguish Gabriel. He and Alexandre had been friends since they were boys, and so Evelyne had always known Gabriel in a distant kind of way. She knew Alexandre trusted Gabriel implicitly, though they were as different as night and day. A point in Gabriel's favor.

She had gone through phases of fascination with him, but she hadn't seen him in Alis for at least a year if not longer, and all her male infatuation had been on Jordi in that time.

Jordi. Had he ever loved her? Would anyone ever love her? And would she even care if there wasn't marriage to a sadistic general on the other side of that?

She hated that she wasn't sure. That it felt now like she'd simply convinced herself to love Jordi. Because it had been a choice she could make, a hope she could have. Was it about wanting *something*? Or was it about wanting *Jordi*?

She hated the answer almost as much as she hated him rejecting running away with her.

"Does Alexandre love Ines?" Evelyne asked abruptly, because she assumed Gabriel would know. Maybe he wouldn't tell her, but he would know.

Gabriel did not answer right away. He pulled her around another corner of shrubbery, under an arbor that somehow smelled of spring though winter was on its way.

"It is not something he has spoken of, one way or another," he said at length.

Evelyne was not sure if he sounded distracted because he was or because he was trying to lie. Though a nonanswer was hardly a lie.

"I hope he does. At least a little bit. I hope she can be a bright spot."

"I hope so too."

She looked up at him then, surprised to find that his voice sounded…at least somewhat earnest. But she shouldn't be surprised. If there was one thing she knew, it was that Alexandre and Gabriel cared for one another like brothers. She'd always thought that Gabriel might be the sole person in the world who knew Alexandre's inner troubles—because he made sure their father didn't, and he didn't want to worry Evelyne with them.

It was dark where they were now. She couldn't make out Gabriel's expression at all, but his hand was still hooked in her arm. He stopped their forward progress, so they stood in the dark, the only sound the rustle of the breeze and their own breathing for a few moments.

Everything suddenly felt odd and tense, when Gabriel was usually the life of the party. Not serious and silent like her brother.

"Gabriel—"

"Shh." His hand curled around hers so that they were *holding hands*.

What on earth was going on?

"Come," he said, his voice low and sensual in her ear. "We must hurry now."

Hurry?

He pulled her along, and she had to all but jog in the painful heels to keep up with him, because for a moment she didn't know what else to do but obey. Maybe she was just too used to obeying.

When he finally came to a stop, it was at a car. She blinked at it, even as he dropped her hand and opened the passenger door and gestured for her to get in. When she didn't move, he crossed back to her and pulled her along.

"Get in the car, Evelyne."

It felt suddenly…threatening or sinister. Why did he want to get her into a car? What was this about? She pulled at his hold, but he did not let her go.

Twin but opposite feelings fluttered low in her stomach. A seed of fear, a sparkle of interest. But since hope was dead, she figured she should listen to the fear. When had she ever been able to trust a man who wasn't her brother anyway? Men, it seemed, were all the same. Maybe even Alexandre was underneath it all, and she only didn't see it because she was his sister.

"Unhand me, Gabriel," she ordered.

He did not. "Do as you're told, Evelyne," he said in

a quiet, authoritative tone she'd never once heard from Gabriel.

She lifted her chin, stopped trying to pull her hand from his grasp, and used all her royal training to sound threatening. "My brother will kill you if you take advantage of me."

Gabriel muttered something in Italian, though she couldn't make it out. It reminded her that while he was *from* Alis, he had spent much of his adolescence and all of his adult life in Italy. Free from Alis and her father.

Free.

And friends with her brother, who she had no reason to doubt. No reason to distrust, male or not. Alexandre had been nothing but a protector in every sense of the word, and it was a sad state of affairs indeed if she let Father, the general and *Jordi* change her sturdy belief in her brother.

"I am not taking advantage of you," he ground out, though he did not loosen his grip. "If you have any sense at all, you'll get in the car."

He glared down at her in the dim light of the palace garage.

He was really quite handsome, particularly in a scowl, which she wasn't sure she'd ever seen on him. It heightened his angular features, did interesting things to his mouth.

Before Jordi, she'd tried her hand at flirting with Gabriel on occasion. He was so *tall*. And he was a man who smiled. No one in the palace ever smiled. Not a real smile.

She thought Gabriel Marti might be the only man she'd ever met who was actually *happy*.

He was not happy now, and she didn't understand why, or what he was doing. Why was he trying to get her in a car? She looked around. No guards. No one watching. If Gabriel could actually get her off the palace property, she could…

She had no idea, but she got in the car all the same on that little spurt of hope that maybe, just maybe, on the other side of this lay freedom. One little sparkle of hope, that Gabriel might in fact be like her brother, might in fact do something that allowed her the freedom she was desperate for.

Gabriel climbed into the driver's seat. He pushed a button and the car started—quietly, almost silently. Then, he began to drive. Toward the palace exit. She looked behind them.

Just twinkling lights surrounded by darkness. The shining lights of the palace getting dimmer and dimmer. No headlights. No shadowy guards dashing after them.

She was afraid to hope. Hope was dead. Except Gabriel was fanning a little ember back to life. "We're escaping?"

"Yes. To a new life, Evelyne. Courtesy of your brother. So if you'd stop arguing with me at every turn and behave, perhaps we could actually save you."

He drove without being followed. It was a positive, but not certain freedom. Not just yet.

He couldn't go to the royal airport without being found out, but if he could get across the border into France, there was a small regional airport not far. His connections outside of Alis were legion, so he already had a plane waiting for them that could not be traced to him or Alexandre.

But he had to make that border crossing first, something that would have been fine if he didn't have a princess in tow. Luckily, he'd always had a backup plan in case King Enzo had decided to try to keep him in the country, or if Alex needed a quick escape. And it had started years ago, when Alex had convinced King Enzo to hire Gabriel's fledgling company to design the wall around the country and some of its security features.

The argument had been that with a novice security design and logistics company like Gabriel's, an Alis native, the king would be wholly in control, with no competing clients to take away focus.

It had been true at the time. And it had given Gabriel the opportunity to design in some…fail-safes.

Maintaining a casual and unsuspicious speed, Gabriel pulled off onto the little-known dirt road that would take him up beyond the border checkpoints. Because there was a point up here where no one knew that Gabriel would be able to get through, car, princess and all, no border checks necessary.

"Gabriel, where are we going?"

"Don't you trust me, *principessa*?"

She sighed heavily. "Alex trusts you, so I will endeavor to, but how are we going to leave Alis if we are just following the border? We will need to go through border patrol, and they will never let me through. Even if Father isn't aware I've run away yet, they won't let me through."

"I have my ways. Relax."

She laughed. Bitterly. "Yes, it's been quite a relaxing day."

He was not sure, despite her upbringing, he'd ever heard *bitterness* from Evelyne. It must have been a family trait, because Alexandre was rarely bitter either. Stern, stoic, determined, but not bitter.

Evelyne was usually cheerful, bubbly, full of…life or hope or something. It was easy to be drawn to Evelyne.

Which was why he needed to get her situated some-where quickly—so he could resume his distance over being *drawn*. She had all the marks of someone who could pull him under, and he would never be pulled under again.

He took an almost unmarked pathway into snow and coaxed the car toward the wall.

Evelyne shifted in her seat, leaning forward, squinting at the wall the headlights of his car illuminated.

"Wait here."

He got out of the car, strode to the wall. With the flash-light of his phone, it only took a minute or two to find the hidden control panel. Alex was lucky Gabriel traveled with a screwdriver on his key chain. Or he was lucky. Or Evelyne was.

He unscrewed the necessary components, hit the cor-rect order of buttons, then replaced the cover and screwed it tight. There was an easily pushed button on the other side to close it.

He heard the engine inside engage, though it rattled a bit. It hadn't been used since Gabriel had tested it when he'd first installed it himself all those years ago. Hope-fully it still worked.

He got back into the car, rubbing his hands against the cold.

"What are we going to do?" Evelyne demanded. "Drive through the…" She trailed off as the motorized entryway he'd designed began to move, open. With enough space he would be able to drive the car right through.

The terrain would be rough on the other side, but it would get them into France undetected.

Evelyne was uncharacteristically silent as he drove through the opening in the wall, stopping the car, then getting out to push the button that would close it. Even when he started driving again after waiting for the door to close—this time with no road or path—she didn't say a word.

But he could all but *hear* the wheels turning in her head.

"Does Alexandre know about that?" she asked once he'd finally maneuvered the car back onto a road—this time on French soil.

"In a way."

"What does *that* mean?"

"He knows I designed some…escape routes into the wall, should they ever be needed. But to protect himself, and no doubt me, he doesn't know exactly where they are. I would of course give him the information should he request it. Instead, he tasked me with getting you out undetected, so here we are."

She said nothing else, all the way to the airport. He supposed she was working through the implications of what escape really meant. Not just a vacation or a lark, but something a little bit dangerous, and a lot life-changing.

Her father was a vindictive man, and she'd never lived anywhere but the palace. Though Alexandre had been sent to boarding school and royal training throughout Europe, Evelyne had been educated in the palace under her father's patriarchal views that a woman did not need worldly experience.

Gabriel arrived at the airport and parked the car where his associate had instructed—an associate who was not supposed to own or operate said plane, so certainly wouldn't go telling anyone that Gabriel had borrowed it.

In the hangar, Gabriel parked out of the way of the plane, turned off the car engine, then got out. Evelyne did not wait for him to come open her door. She got out of the car and eyed the plane.

"I suppose we will need to wait for daylight to fly."

"Not necessarily. What we *will* need to wait for is me to return to the castle."

She whirled to face him. "What?"

"Only briefly. To make an appearance so no one suspects *I* am the one who absconded with you as I was the last one seen with you. I'll drop a word to the guards that you voluntarily left with a shadowy figure. And I was distracted by another young lady. Something along those lines." He flashed her a grin. "Easy enough to be believed."

Evelyne's eyebrows drew together as she thought this over. Then her eyes narrowed.

"Tell them it was Jordi Ferriz. Not a shadowy figure. An aide."

He found her fervor suspicious. "That would put a target on this Jordi's back."

She lifted a regal chin. "Good."

Ah, some sort of...lovers' tiff, he thought. He did not know this aide named Jordi, but he did know something about revenge. And what it did to you. "Vengeance is a dangerous game, *principessa*."

She lifted a bare shoulder, and Gabriel might have been frustrated with her, except he was too distracted by *her*.

The dress was a torture device, Gabriel was quite certain. It skimmed every curve, something about the green color seemed to gild her skin with gold. A gold that reflected in little flecks in her dark eyes.

And he did not have any clothes for her to change into on the plane. He couldn't risk grabbing something of hers at the palace to bring back. He wouldn't be there long, with any luck. Just a quick appearance, a word to the guards, then off again.

"Get on the plane. Wait for me there. I will be back in under an hour." Hopefully.

She met his gaze. There was trepidation there, but she nodded and allowed herself to be helped up into the plane.

She hesitated at the top of the stairs. "Gabriel… Are you sure…" But she didn't finish that sentence.

"Would you rather return to the palace, Evelyne?"

She immediately shook her head. "No, I cannot stay. I cannot marry the general."

"No, you can't. Your brother agrees. So we will find a new life for you."

"What about Alexandre?"

"Alex is the only one who has any hope of surviving your father's reign, especially after marrying Ines. I think he knows this as well as you and I do."

Evelyne let out a shaky sigh. Gabriel took it as agreement and turned to leave, but Evelyne reached out, her slim hand curling around his hand.

"What if Father punishes Alexandre? What if…?"

"He won't," Gabriel said with more force than he actually believed, but she needed reassurance, and he supposed he did as well. "First, your father needs his son, his heir. If he didn't, Alex would have been punished with much worse long ago. Second, Alex will not know where you are, just that I have taken you somewhere safe.

There will be no evidence connecting you to him, so while your father could *decide* to blame him, he can't prove it. He won't want to prove it. He'll probably make up some boogeyman who stole you. Send General Vinyes on a wild-goose chase."

"I suppose you're right." She chewed on her bottom lip, a distracting and brain-draining move that distracted him enough to meet her golden gaze. "What if he punishes *you*?" she asked, eyes worried, voice soft. "What if the chase is General Vinyes to us?"

"Do you underestimate me, Evelyne?" he quipped, but her eyes were wide and shiny as she studied him.

He had never seen Evelyne look vulnerable. He knew, from Alex, that the king was especially hard on her, but Alex had always been vague about what that meant. And Evelyne never seemed to be troubled. Sociable, confident, cheeky even.

He saw the troubled in her now.

"Everything will be all right," he assured her, with an odd gentleness from himself he did not quite recognize. "You have my word."

So he left her there, determined to see his word through.

CHAPTER THREE

EVELYNE WAITED FOR Gabriel's return, trying not to fret and failing. Her father *was* a vindictive man, and even if Gabriel somehow managed to pull this off, Father would look for someone to blame.

Who would be harmed because of it? Perhaps it had been vindictive and petty to want to name Jordi. Maybe she was more like her father than she'd want to admit. She almost hoped Gabriel would ignore her there.

Almost.

Unfortunately, the only other option to this one would be to return to the castle and marry a man as evil as her father.

Impossible. She had to take the freedom Alexandre had arranged for her.

That Gabriel would put himself in the line of fire for her—no, not *her*, for Alex—was a surprise. And now she was curious just what would indebt the man to her brother so much. She was quite sure Gabriel had built his own wealth and success with no help from Alex.

But surely just being good friends wouldn't be enough for Gabriel to risk life and limb to do all *this*. And surely her brother would not have asked it of Gabriel if there was not something…more to this.

But what? She couldn't even come up with an idea.

She did not have her phone. She did not have a jacket. She had nothing except this dress suitable for a princess at a royal wedding, heels that felt too tight and painful to put back on and the sloshing feeling of nothing but champagne being in her stomach.

And Gabriel was going to be gone for at least an hour.

She dozed. Probably ill-advisedly considering she was alone in a strange plane in a deserted hangar, but the events of the day had just completely sapped her energy, and the low-level nausea wasn't helping. So she reclined back in the comfortable plane seat and slept.

When she opened her eyes, not quite remembering that she'd fallen asleep and certainly not sure how long she'd been out, she was not alone anymore.

She might have startled at direct hazel eyes clearly having been watching her, but there was something very centering about Gabriel. Like an anchor amid this very strange and unexpected storm.

He moved toward her. "Here." He handed her a bag. "Just things I could pick up along the way. Some guests of the palace will wonder where their things went, but I'm certain they'll get over it."

Evelyne shook her sleep- and champagne-foggy mind and unzipped the bag. She pulled out a man's coat—too small to be Gabriel's. Some kind of faux fur shawl. A pair of slippers—she was so excited about those she immediately shoved them onto her feet.

She let out a sigh of relief.

"Now, eat while I prepare to take off." This time, he set a kind of bakery box in her lap. She opened it, saw an array of bits and pieces from the wedding meal and reception food.

Her stomach sloshed in protest. "I don't feel so well."

"Eat," he insisted. "That will help." He turned, walking up the aisle toward the cockpit of the plane.

"Where are you going?"

He glanced over his shoulder at her. His hair was more disheveled now, and he'd lost the suit jacket somewhere along the way. His smile was rakish. "Someone needs to fly this, don't they?"

"And that someone is *you*?" She gripped the bakery box and leaned forward. "Gabriel, please don't tell me you're one of those men who thinks he can fly a plane simply because you're good with machines."

His mouth curved in amusement. "It might be enjoyable to let you think that, but no, Evelyne. I have a license and everything. I imagine there is *much* about me that would surprise you. Now eat." He nodded at the box in her lap then disappeared into the cockpit.

He could fly a plane. There was indeed much about Gabriel that would no doubt surprise her. Everything about this night would be included in that list.

She was used to taking orders, so she felt compelled to do as she was told. She surveyed the offerings of the bakery box.

A few of the puff pastry appetizers that weren't too appetizing this many hours on. Two rolls. And most importantly, a piece of wedding cake, wrapped up to protect the frosting.

She ate that first, though it probably wasn't her best choice. Still, she'd been dreaming about this cake all week. Ines had impeccable taste in baked goods. Once she was satisfied on a taste level, she forced herself to eat the rest.

The plane lurched, and so did the food in her stomach, but she closed her eyes and breathed through it. The nausea *and* the knowledge that Gabriel was the one taxiing the plane out of the hangar. Onto a runway.

The sun was peeking over the horizon, painting the sky in blush pinks and oranges. Evelyne decided to take it as a good omen. As hope.

Hope was back. Freedom was here.

That spurt of joy was fleeting as they traveled. It would seem she'd doze off just as they arrived somewhere new and switched planes. At one point, they even had a private room on a railcar. Gabriel had presented her with a large meal there, and a shopping bag. Inside were silly tourist clothes—but anything was better than someone else's coat and the godforsaken royal dress. The best part were the sneakers—a step up from the slippers she'd been schlepping around in.

When they boarded yet another private plane, Gabriel once again in the pilot's seat, she was perilously close to crying. She didn't know how many hours, *days* it had been. She'd wanted escape, but she wasn't sure how much she had left in her. Which no doubt made her weak.

"This will be the last one," he told her gently. "We will have a bit of a drive once we land, but this is the last flight."

Evelyne seated herself in the copilot's seat. "Where are we going?"

He looked at all the dials and whatnot, didn't even spare her a glance. "The States. A new continent seems safest."

A new continent. A new life. Away from everything she'd ever known. The palace, her father. She was free… But at the cost of everything. Including… Alexandre. Would she ever see him again?

The thought brought a stab of pain, and tears to her eyes she was afraid she wouldn't be able to fight if she stayed in that thought. "I know nothing about America," she said instead of, *will I ever see Alex again?* She was afraid if she voiced that, she might fall apart completely.

"You know how to speak English. That should be enough."

Evelyne did not know *how* speaking the language would be enough. It had been one thing to insist Jordi run away with her, it was something altogether different to actually think about the practicalities of what running away meant.

She had been raised a princess in a small, isolated country. While she had suffered monstrous punishments at the hand of her father, she had also been waited on and pampered in other ways.

What would she do in America? How would she survive without Alexandre's protection and guidance? It seemed unsurmountable.

And still, this horrible, terrifying unsurmountable was better than marrying the general. *Everything* was better than that, and she reminded herself of this again and again while Gabriel once again guided a small plane into the sky, taking her far away from the monsters that had stalked her pampered life.

Maybe somewhere between the two extremes lay a life worth living.

* * *

Gabriel was glad she was sleeping, even if he was concerned about the amount she'd done since this whole thing started two days ago now. She'd had a traumatic event. Sleep was good. He wished she'd eat more. Once he got her settled, he'd insist upon it.

He drove up the curving driveway to the home he'd procured for her. He'd had to pull some considerable strings to get a house off the market with no connection to him, but the thing about designing and implementing security systems for the rich and powerful was that he had just the kind of connections that could keep things… *off the books*.

He'd considered going small, rustic. Some tiny, rural town no one would ever expect to find a princess in, but Evelyne would not know how to survive *rustic*, and he doubted very much she could fit in *with* rustic. Since Gabriel could not yet afford to risk hiring staff for her that might wonder who the regal beauty was, he thought procuring something she was better used to was the better bet.

So he'd gone with the grand *and* isolated. The rugged Maine coast boasted some beautiful homes, spread out and situated far away from any metropolitan center. The mansion he had procured for her stood on a sea cliff overlooking the crashing Atlantic. He could not staff it yet, until he found someone trustworthy and who had no chance of discovering who Evelyne really was. So she would be all by herself in all that space.

She would no doubt not find this ideal, but escape— even well-funded escape—did not always get to be ideal.

He turned the vehicle off, and this must have woken

her, because she blinked her eyes open, straightened in the seat, gazing out the windshield at the grand house spread out before them, the ocean in the distance.

"Welcome home, Evelyne."

She didn't say anything, so he got out of the car and skirted the hood to open her door for her. He even helped her out. Her gaze stayed glued to the ocean beyond the house.

"Gabriel…" Her eyes were wide. "This is… Is this yours?"

"No, it is Francesco Marino's. He's an eccentric Italian billionaire—a false identity I have used before when needed. Now he has a young wife, Lina, and they have hermited themselves away in America to enjoy their newly found wedded bliss." He made a grand sweeping gesture to encompass the house and sea.

He enjoyed the stories, creating them, implementing them. In his business, it paid to have an identity or two that had no connection to who he really was. Both for himself and sometimes his clients.

"Locals will occasionally catch a glimpse of one of them on the balconies," he continued. "But never in town. The nearest town could never meet their extravagant needs anyhow."

"But… Even with these fake identities, you bought this, you paid for it, you…"

"Have no worries, Evelyne, I can certainly afford it," he said dryly. "And a land holding, even under a fake identity, is never a bad thing to have."

"It's so big. It's so…much." She shook her head. "Are you to stay with me?" she asked.

"Not for long. It is too dangerous. I must return to Italy and work as soon as possible, before King Enzo starts concerning himself with my whereabouts. But I will stay long enough to get you settled, under the guise of being out of contact range on a job in Moscow. Now, you are not to have any contact with Alexandre, or anyone back in Alis, but either of you can contact *me* and I will act as careful conduit. But I would relegate this only to emergencies, Evelyne. This is very delicate." He began to lead her toward the house. "I will visit on occasion, to take care of whatever necessities arise, but it must be done carefully, so it will be infrequent. Eventually, we will hire you some staff, but for now, you will have to make do on your own."

He pulled the key he'd procured in New York from his pocket, unlocked the front door and gestured her inside.

She stepped in, a bit like someone suffering some kind of shock. Like she didn't quite know how to put one foot in front of the other.

"It is yours, essentially, for the time being. As long as your father searches for you, it will be your home and refuge."

She turned in a circle in the soaring foyer, white and a bit bland. The whole house was rather commercial and bland feeling.

Evelyne's dark, gold-flecked gaze met his. "Why are you doing this? I know you and Alex are friends, best friends, but this is…above and beyond friendship."

He considered just what to tell her. This *was* above and beyond, and while he liked to think of himself as a good man, now that Alex had put him on that path, he would not have gone to *such* lengths for anyone else. Though he liked to think he would have gone to *some* lengths to help a young woman escape what would no doubt become an abusive situation.

Still, the truth of his bond with Alexandre, the truth of *him*, was not something he shared with anyone. But there was a way of phrasing anything that left people thinking they knew the answer to something, even if they didn't.

It was how he'd lived his adult life, skating the surface of any real connections. Anything that might threaten to pull him under again.

"Years ago, I almost made a very grave mistake," Gabriel said conversationally, walking through the foyer and into one of the sitting rooms, knowing she'd follow. The furniture here was almost cozy, though still too much white to be a welcoming room. "One that would have ended my life—literally or figuratively, one way or another. Your brother was the one who stopped me. He saved me—and had to fight tooth and nail to do it—and I owe him for this."

"So this is your payment?" she asked carefully.

"It is my thank-you gift." He corrected her, because friendship did not require payment, to his way of thinking. He gestured at the window, which was the entire length of the wall. It looked out over the crashing ocean below.

Evelyne stepped to the glass. The cloudy light gave her an ethereal glow, even with the silly sweatsuit emblazoned with mountains and *Interlaken* in looping script. She would need a wardrobe, a way to get groceries without being seen, little things like that to keep her well the next few weeks while he made sure nothing connected him to her disappearance or her to Maine.

She all but pressed her nose to the window, clearly delighted by the view. Which gave him a satisfaction he did not wish to think too deeply on.

"Sometimes I wonder if he's really as good as he seems to me. Can anyone be that saintly?"

There could only be one *he* she was referring to. "Sometimes I wonder this myself. He has always seemed…otherworldly, almost, in his determination to the right thing. If he was a terrible man, like your father, I could understand it. His *right thing* wouldn't be right at all, if he was like the king. But he understands real right, and insists it be done. I do not know how, but he *is* good."

"I think it must have come from my mother," she said quietly. "He was almost eight years old when she died. He remembers her. She must have taught him." Evelyne looked back at him as if hoping he could confirm this.

But he could not. While Gabriel remembered their mother in a vague kind of way, he had moved away from Alis about a year before the queen had died. On top of that, there were subjects Alexandre never broached. No matter what.

His mother was one of them.

"Well, I do not know how to thank you, Gabriel. Even if you've done this for Alex, you have taken great pains to do something that will benefit me." She reached out, took his hands in hers and gave them a squeeze. It was a very royal move, but the warmth of her small hands, the warmth of her words…they had an effect on him, royal or no.

The gold in her eyes, the fervency in her voice seemed to spread a heating warmth through him. That alluring temptation he had little experience resisting, because what temptation couldn't he indulge in?

Her. Her. Her.

"You have saved me," she said, her voice rough. "I owe you everything."

Uncomfortable with a great many things, he pulled his hands from hers, stepped back. "I do not require thanks. Come, let us see what we can scrounge up to eat." He turned on a heel and walked out of the living room in search of the kitchen. He had seen the floor plan of the house, so he had a vague idea where everything was.

Another thing he would do with the days he could afford to stay was ensure her security system was state of the art. The best Marti Systems had to offer.

While he kept her from touching him, even so generically, ever again.

The kitchen was big. Everything seemed commercial grade. Still with that almost corporate feeling. Perhaps once some time passed, he could have it redecorated, give the place some warmth for her.

"I'm afraid all this will be lost on me," Evelyne said, peering down at the stainless-steel gas stove. "Father often punished me with cleaning tasks, but I was never much allowed in the kitchens. I'm not even sure I know how to make toast."

"Lucky for you, the internet is a trove of information that can teach you. Definitely how to make toast. I have already had the fridge and pantry stocked for you prior to our arrival, and we'll set up recurring grocery deliveries in some way before I leave."

"I don't have my phone, my computer…" She looked around, clearly a bit overwhelmed by everything, and understandably so. "I don't have anything."

"It'll all be taken care of before I leave."

"Leave." She wrinkled her nose, but she turned away from him so he only caught the hint of her profile. "What will I do in this big house all by myself?" she asked, hugging her arms around herself.

"Stay out of sight. Live a quiet, private life. Learn to cook, perhaps." He shrugged. "That is up to you, how you spend your time. Such is freedom."

"How novel." She delivered the quip with a hint of humor, a hint of self-deprecating sarcasm. "I am not sure anything of importance has ever been up to me. I am not sure I know how to…handle things being up to me."

"Freedom always comes with a bit of a price and learning curve, I fear."

She nodded, straightened her shoulders. She looked older than she had. Not quite duller, but not as *shiny* was the only word he could think of.

"Well, I'm ready to pay it," she said resolutely.

He felt strangely proud and figured it best if he didn't linger on that feeling.

CHAPTER FOUR

THE DAY EVELYNE dreaded had come. After just three days of getting her settled, Gabriel would leave her here. Alone.

She *almost* loved the house. It was beautiful, if a little overly white and almost sterile feeling inside, but she absolutely loved standing on the balconies, terraces and porches watching the sea's fascinating dance. Sometimes the lull of calm waves against the rock, sometimes angry slaps, sometimes chaotic whirls. It made up for the bad decorating.

She would have loved the house itself, she thought, if it was full of people—like the palace had been. But the echoing emptiness of it at night—with Gabriel the entire length of the home away—left her uneasy and...sad.

Sadness was silly, she knew. She had escaped her father and General Vinyes. This was cause for constant happiness and celebration. She should be *ecstatic*.

But really, she'd traded one prison for another. Gabriel even warned her against taking walks just yet. And now he was leaving her alone and with instructions to stay inside.

This prison was *better* of course. No one would beat her or ridicule her or force her to marry a man who would also no doubt beat and ridicule her, but it was still...forced solitary confinement—even if the confinement was elegant and luxurious.

Gabriel must have read her distress over that—he was good at *reading* the room. Or just her. And not in the way her father or even Alexandre was. Though she hated to draw comparisons between her father and brother, they both had a way of understanding her in order to *maneuver* her into whatever they wanted.

But what Alex wanted was for the greater good, so that was not so bad. What her father wanted was always to prove his power, his dominance, so that *was* bad.

But Gabriel seemed to read her in order to...understand. And now, he assuaged her concerns. Or tried to.

"Eventually, we will ease your way into a less isolated life," he was saying while she watched him fiddle with a computer—*her* computer now. He'd gotten all sorts of things in place over the past three days. A computer, a phone, an entire security system controlled by both. "Once the talk of your disappearance dies down, once your father finds some different vengeance plot to follow, and with some slight physical details shifted, you may eventually lead a very normal life."

May. Eventually. She tried not to be depressed by those words—she was safe from both her father *and* the general, after all. She was *lucky*.

She would teach herself to cook. She would watch the ocean. Maybe at some point she could buy some paint, some new furniture, bring life to this place's interior.

And she would do all of these things without being manipulated, ridiculed or beaten. Ever again.

"Grocery delivery is set up, just as I showed you, without any personal contact. I have left you a document full of instructions for the security system. It should answer any query. You are not to contact me unless it is a dire emergency."

She nodded, not trusting her voice. She didn't want him to go. She'd come to realize she enjoyed his company. He was charming, funny, and that bright smile was like sunlight after years in shadows.

And in Gabriel, she saw everything Jordi had let her believe about him that hadn't been true at all. Gabriel saw things through. He had no fear. He had *risked* for her. Well, for Alexandre.

She could trust Gabriel to protect her, just as Alexandre had always protected her. Even if he left. He had done *all* this, at great risk to himself. Regardless of the reason, he was brave. Strong. Admirable.

She would miss him. Desperately.

Gabriel studied her. Saw through her, she could tell. "I will come back to check on you in a few weeks," he said gently.

She felt as though she might cry. Or fall down at his feet and beg him to stay. She *refused* to do either. At least in front of him, but it didn't stop her from being a little bit pathetic. "Do you promise?"

"You have a state-of-the-art security system in place if you are worried about safety. I will make certain no one from Alis finds you. I promise you, just as I promised your brother."

"I'm not afraid. Not like that. I just…" She looked around the room. "It will all just be so empty. I have never really been alone before. Not like this."

"Then enjoy it, Evelyne." He gave her shoulder a brotherly kind of pat. "I'll be back in a few weeks. You have my word."

And he kept it. Every few weeks, Gabriel would appear with no notice. Usually in the dead of night. She would get a little notification on her phone, waking her up, and she would let him in the back door.

In the shadows of those nights, Evelyne felt her heart race. The sound of his voice would drift along her skin like a delicious secret. The scent of him would find itself in little spaces around her house, and even though he stayed in a bedroom on the other side of the house, she slept easier every night he was here.

The first trip he arrived with hair bleach, which she hadn't been able to bring herself to use. She didn't think she was *vain*, but she liked her hair the way it was, and if she wasn't leaving the house, what was the point of changing her appearance?

He had *laughed* at her, but not in a mean way. As though he was just amused by her.

"Well, keep it around, for the future."

She spent the weeks in between his appearances trying to keep herself entertained. Gabriel had suggested she enjoy some alone time, and while she enjoyed being able to do whatever she wished around the house whenever she wished, it was still a very small life.

And she missed people. She missed Alexandre. How was Ines settling into the palace? Would they be introducing a baby soon? A baby she'd never get to meet?

Thoughts like that made her incredibly sad, or would start a spiral of thoughts... Was her father mistreating Ines? Would he mistreat a grandchild? Especially if Alexandre and Ines ended up having a girl?

Or was he so obsessed with her disappearance—something that would no doubt haunt him as a symbol of his lack of power—that eventually he'd track her down and find her?

But every time she got to *that* thought, she reminded herself to breathe. If there was anyone in this world she thought could keep her safe and hidden from her father, it was Gabriel.

So in the weeks between his visits, she threw herself into whatever projects she could think of. Mostly, she worked on teaching herself to cook, via those internet videos Gabriel had suggested. She tried to not think of the palace, of Alis. Instead, she simply tried to survive.

When Gabriel appeared next, almost two full months from their escape, she had a meal all planned out. She put it together while he locked himself in one of the office rooms and talked to someone on the phone in a language she didn't know.

She had spent weeks upon weeks watching cooking videos, and while there'd been a few fails along the way, she was starting to get the hang of it. She was proud of the meal she'd made Gabriel, and the pretty little dining room scene she'd created—complete with flower arrangement and candlelight.

She was even more proud when he strode into the dining room and stopped short, like he couldn't quite believe what he saw.

He blinked once, then carefully swept that surprised expression away. He smiled. "Look at you. I suppose you can teach an old dog new tricks."

She rolled her eyes at the idea of being *old*. "It's fun."

She thought of the pile of dishes in the kitchen sink that would be her responsibility and hers alone. "Sort of."

She'd set the table family style, with plates set next to each other so he couldn't try to sit all the way down the table like he had last time. She hated the huge, ugly, black, shiny table so she'd scrounged up an elaborate silk tablecloth. Still not to her tastes, but better than *black*.

Gabriel took his seat, and she took the one next to him. She watched him with a growing fascination. He did not treat her like he treated other women. She was pretty sure she'd seen him harmlessly *flirt* with anyone from the age of five to ninety-five. It was just *him*, and the way he moved through a crowd. Charming, happy, easy.

Except with her. He kept himself a little…tense, a little…closed off. Not that he wasn't charming, exactly, but he was…stiffer, she supposed.

Evelyne had spent an inordinate time deciding what that meant. What else did she have to do? Learning to cook and cleaning up after didn't take up full weeks at a time.

"I think I should like some paint," she told Gabriel, as he usually restocked anything she needed on his little visits. "Some new furniture. I'd like to make some of these rooms at least a little but more…cozy."

"Write me out a detailed list. We'll figure it out."

She smiled. "You're too good to me."

His smile was…tight. She studied it now, then picked up the glass of wine she'd already poured, sipped. He gave it a fleeting glance, before his eyes moved to his own untouched glass, then his plate.

"Is something wrong?" she asked. She didn't think there was, and she also knew he wouldn't tell her if there was, but she wanted…something. A reaction? A blip? To be able to read this way he dealt with her.

"Everything is going according to plan," he said. "Your father has told the press that he has a 'suspect' in your disappearance."

"Who?" Evelyne demanded, setting the wineglass down a bit too hard. Worry spiraled through her. Did Father suspect Alexandre? Gabriel?

Gabriel lifted a shoulder, cutting through the chicken in a lemon cream sauce. "He's keeping it quite tight-lipped, which makes me believe it's a story to save face. If he has *no* idea what happened to you, he looks like a fool." He took a bite, nodded approvingly. "So he's invented this 'suspect.' With any luck, he'll invent a story that makes everyone think you're dead."

How odd for that to be counted as luck.

She looked down at her plate, poked at the chicken as dread and the deflation of any wisp of happiness took up residence in her stomach. "He'll never stop looking for me." She knew this deep in her bones. The idea of her somehow tricking him, escaping him would not be one he'd ever get over. Gabriel would and could protect her, she had no doubts.

But would it require her to live like this always?

"No," Gabriel agreed in that easy way of his. "But I think he might tell the country you were murdered. He hasn't yet, but it's a rumbling. He'll keep looking, since he knows you weren't, and it'll never sit right with him that you escaped, but if he's the only one looking… It makes things easier for us."

He lifted his hand, and for a moment, she thought he'd

put it over hers. Instead, he reached for his wine. Took a drink.

A very large drink. What was that about?

She watched him eat, thought about it as he easily led the conversation around to a wide variety of topics. It was not a surprise, exactly, that he was so intelligent, so well-versed in so many things. He was a wealthy, privileged man.

But he spoke to her…like an equal. She hadn't fully realized how rare that was until this moment. Her brother had a…paternal way of dealing with her, which she'd never minded overmuch. He had been her protector for her whole life, and she had certainly spent a lot of time wishing *he* was her father.

The staff treated her in much the same way, even the well-meaning ones who were simply scared of her father, not loyal to him in that way. Her life had always been an odd extreme of privilege and punishment.

But the way Gabriel asked questions about what she knew, what she thought, made her realize that even Jordi had treated her a bit like a child who couldn't possibly have opinions of her own.

The thought depressed her. It spoke to desperation, she supposed, that she'd believed his seduction had been love, simply because he had given her any attention.

Gabriel nudged her plate. "You need to eat, Evelyne."

"You are the only one who has ever concerned themselves with if I do not eat."

"I'm sure that isn't true."

"I'm sure you'd be wrong," she muttered, poking the chicken with her fork, then forgoing the food for another sip of wine. She studied him, didn't bother to hide it through sideways glances or anything else.

"Father used to punish me if I ate too much," she said conversationally. She supposed she had to admit that some of her food issues stemmed from trauma right there. "Or if I did not like something I was supposed to. Or if I made a mess of things. A princess should eat small portions and do it prettily," she recited.

She looked up, vaguely amused at how *silly* it all seemed, but the expression on Gabriel's face was not what she expected. She had not been sure what to expect, but certainly not *rage*.

She swallowed, surprised that the fury she saw there did not frighten her, did not remind her of being in her father's office, but instead seemed to hit her bloodstream like alcohol—a burning, freeing, *fizzing* wave of what could only be termed as desire.

That someone might actually be…angry on her behalf. Not because they were related, but because it had… harmed her. She knew that everything Gabriel did was because Alexandre was his friend, but being *angry* on her behalf was something…else.

Something about *her*.

"Your father is a scourge," Gabriel said darkly, but she saw the way he was fighting back the severity of his reaction. He breathed carefully, unclenched the hand that had balled up into a fist.

He was a fascinating man, so many little pockets of emotion and reaction. So different from her brother, whose stoicism bordered on a total lack of personality.

It made her wonder. She understood that so much of

what Gabriel had done was a thank you to Alexandre, but she still existed. She breathed. She was involved.

And he was angry at her father on her behalf.

"What do you think of me, Gabriel?"

He raised an eyebrow, took a sip of his wine before responding. "That is a leading question."

"Indeed. Answer it anyway."

His mouth curved, ever so slightly. "You are not a princess here, Evelyne. And I am not your subject to order about."

"Well, you are wrong on half of that," she replied, grinning at him in humor. "America and fake identities or not, I am *always* a princess."

That curve of his mouth turned into a full-blown smile in return, the rage and anger gone. This had a similar effect though, a beautiful fluttering in her chest, spreading warmth through her body. Like a...blooming.

"Fair enough, *principessa*. What do I think of you?" He speared a piece of chicken with his fork. "You are impressive, Evelyne. This is delicious, and while you might have had ample time to teach yourself how to cook, not everyone would use their time wisely."

It surprised her, how easily the compliment was delivered. She hesitated, shifted in her seat, not quite sure what to do with *praise*. "Well. I have also spent a lot of time staring off into the ocean."

He shrugged. "Understandable. You have withstood having to leave everything you've ever known behind and exist mostly alone. The surroundings are nice, no doubt, but that doesn't make the process easy. But you have spine. Underneath that sparkle and personality. You

have your brother's strength, or you would not have survived your father."

For a moment, she was rendered completely speechless. Compliments were not something she was used to,
aside from ones about her looks. Anything compliment-
ing her *spine* or *strength* was completely foreign and...
wonderful.

He must have sensed something of the enormity of her
reaction, because he frowned, then shifted in his seat.
Almost as though confident, carefree Gabriel Marti was
uncomfortable.

"Eat three more bites," he ordered, like a parent would
to a child. "Then I will help you clean up your mess."

She thought to argue with him, but eating the somewhat insulting *three more* bites like she was a child and
having him help clean up kept them close.

So she ate a little bit of her chicken while he cleared his
plate. This filled her with satisfaction too. He would not
clear his plate if the food was horrible, even to assuage
her ego. Gabriel was *nice* to her because of Alexandre,
but she did not think he cared all that much about her *ego*.

He cleared the table with her, then moved to the sink.
This was something she had come to the house knowing how to do. One of her punishments as a child for her
many infractions at the dinner table had been to wash all
the dishes for the palace. By hand.

Some of the women in the kitchens had been kind to
her, taught her how to take care of her hands, had tried to
carefully help her, but since everyone was afraid of King
Enzo they had not done her work for her.

"I'll wash, you can dry," she told Gabriel.

"Do you know what this contraption is right here?" he asked, amused, pointing at the dishwasher.

She batted her eyelashes at him. "I thought it was a paper shredder."

"Funny."

Since she *did* know what it was for, and in fact how to use it—she'd even read the manual she'd found in the kitchen drawer to be sure—she handed him a dish towel. "You are meant to handwash these pans, and the knives. The kind women in the kitchens of the palace taught me this. Then, since I already have to do that, I handwash the rest. It's just me. Or me and you, so convenience doesn't really have much of a place here. It gives me something to do."

If he had a reaction to that, she couldn't read it. "Very well." He unbuttoned the cuffs of his shirt, pushed the sleeves up to the elbow.

Evelyne found her gaze trapped there for a moment. She studied the muscular forearms, wondered how he kept in such good shape. Was he some kind of gym rat? His hands spoke of…some kind of physical work. Though his watch was expensive, he had the slash of a faded scar over the back of his left hand.

Would his hands be rough then? What would it feel like to be touched by hands that had seen work outside typing up missives and handling phone calls in the palace? She'd only ever been with Jordi, and not often. It had been…pleasant enough, though she thought most of the enjoyment came from doing something she wasn't supposed to be doing under her father's nose.

Perhaps for both of them.

Gabriel, on the other hand, didn't strike her as a man

who concerned himself with what he was *allowed*. Didn't her entire escape prove that? Not many would go against King Enzo's wishes.

But he had. For Alexandre, yes, but because he was a brave man, a strong man, a smart man.

A handsome man who she knew only in relation to her brother. But he was a good man, or Alexandre would not be friends with him—no matter what stories Gabriel had about being saved by Alex. He was a good man, or he would not have risked so much to bring her here.

She did not know very many good men. If not for Alexandre, she would know none, believe in none.

But she believed in Gabriel. She believed that she could feel freedom and hope in his arms. Because if she could convince him to touch her, kiss her, be with her, that would be for *her*. Not to endure something. Not to save her.

No, it would simply be something to enjoy.

Would he be appalled by her thoughts? Amused? Or was his behavior at dinner, and a few other times over the course of all this, a sign that he might have thoughts along the same lines?

He thought her *strong*.

She wanted him to show her strength. She wanted him to show her a million things. She wanted to feel alive, and independent and *free*. She hadn't yet. As much as this was better than the palace, a life being promised to General Vinyes, it had yet to feel like real, true freedom.

He would feel that way. But how could she make that happen?

There was a moment, brief and exciting, where she handed him a wet pan. He lifted his gaze, and it met hers.

He *must* have realized what was in her gaze—heat, interest, want. And he did not immediately look away or rebuff any of these things.

No, she saw each and every one of those in his own gaze, before he blinked them away.

And made his excuses to leave.

But Evelyne was beginning to formulate a plan. One that involved more than just *gazes* meeting.

CHAPTER FIVE

GABRIEL HAD PLANNED on staying three nights this trip. After that moment in his kitchen, he had his concerns about such a long stay.

Perhaps he should cut it short, just as he'd cut short helping her with kitchen cleanup. He'd leave in the morning with an excuse he'd gotten called away on business.

Cowardly. He was currently lying in a bed an entire length of the house away from where she would be lying in her own bed, arguing with himself over which was worse—a cowardly escape or an impossible temptation.

Would she be thinking of him as he thought of her?

She looked beautiful in candlelight. She looked beautiful in all lights. Her interest or curiosity or, he supposed, *both* wasn't lost on him. And in every under-the-lashes or sideway glance was a potential land mine.

He was not immune—could not seem to find the reserves to *be* immune. Not to Evelyne.

The straight-on look over dishes this evening was more than any land mine. He had seen stark invitation in her eyes, and he wanted to accept. The claws of need had insisted upon it.

Only a strength born of learning of his own potential to destroy gave him the strength to rip those claws out.

He had learned that anything deeper than superficial interest could lead him to the depths of violence and loss of control. Something he could never afford again, especially around someone who had already suffered violence.

He could not touch Evelyne. The obsession would become untenable. It was already too much. He thought of her constantly when he was away. He found every new layer he discovered about her fascinating. Every time he planned his clandestine returns, he was filled with brand-new energy. Anticipation.

He wanted to see her smile, to hear her laugh, to inhale the subtle floral scent that followed her around every room. He wanted. Period. A want that had gotten too large in his mind.

He took some solace in the fact that his obsession with Evelyne hadn't affected his work, but it *had* affected his social life. He had not enjoyed going out since he'd brought her here. Had not been with a woman since he'd gone to Alexandre's wedding. All the surfaces he'd skated across no longer held any distraction for him.

Pathetic. He needed to fix that before he made a larger mistake. Here. With *her*.

He had known she had spine and strength—to come out of a childhood raised by King Enzo and retain any sparkle took an immense capacity for both. And yes, she had Alex to cushion some of her blows, but not all.

But for some years he had kept his distance because he knew that the combination of her was a temptation not just in terms of sex—but in terms of this, the dangerous claws of obsessive *want*. She was beautiful and alluring, but beyond that she was complex, intriguing, intelligent, with some added extra dash of something he could only describe as *fun*.

He got out of bed, frustrated that over ten years of learning how to be a different man seemed to crumble in the face of one woman.

There were threats against her, and he would save her from all of them. Protect her from anything that might touch her.

And he knew that in the depths of this obsession, it could lead him to kill. *That* was inside him. No better than King Enzo, really, except he knew he had to control it.

The room had French doors that led out to a balcony that looked out over the sea, so he opened them and stepped out.

The cold, whipping air and the salty tang of sea hit him like a blow—a welcome one tonight. The little tempest that raged out there felt like solace against his bare skin.

He understood her loneliness. There was something exhilarating and wonderful about the thrashing sea below, but it served as a reminder to him how different her new life was. How he'd plopped her here, yes, to save her, but alone with no one to talk to and with nothing to do but learn how to haunt a house.

She was too skinny. Too…fragile seeming yet. She wouldn't crumble, she had too much spine for that, but she wasn't *thriving*. He told himself that wanting her to thrive was for Alex and Alex alone, but he knew better.

The thought of her being punished for *eating too much*—in a *palace*—boiled his blood. Knowing some of the details of the way King Enzo had abused her—and he had no doubt that only scratched the surface—enraged him.

He had once been enraged on behalf of a woman. And his obsession had led him to a violent outburst that would have resulted in another man's death. Would have, if not for Alexandre.

All these years later, that fire still burned within him—twined with the relief he had been saved from the dangerous poison that had held him in its grip.

He had never allowed himself to dance near that flame again. He skated along, not letting himself get hooked into all that could devolve into the desire to destroy.

But he didn't have a choice now. He'd been named Evelyne's savior, her protector. Just like he'd once named himself a young woman's protector.

He could not sink into those old depths of disaster, but he had yet to figure out a way to extricate himself from this, the *flame* of all Evelyne was.

You don't want to.

He'd seen desire in her eyes, the heat of chemistry. He'd felt it echo through him, a bit like a bomb detonating. Just as he'd known might happen. *Would* happen.

He had learned how to handle his…appetites, desires. It was easy now, to keep the *personal* out of any sexual encounter. Enjoy it for what it was. *Enjoy* had become the cornerstone of his life. A surface level amusement with everything. Nothing mattered enough to obsess over. Nothing mattered enough to fan the fire of vengeance that lived in him—a seed of disaster always searching for a little bit of water and sun.

Nothing could be *surface* with Evelyne. Everything about her was personal. Deeper. A constant, dangerous pitfall. Because he remembered all the times she'd attempted to flirt with him in the past.

All the times he'd been tempted to fall for her alluring smiles and sparkling wit. He'd known then, even as
a young man, to keep his distance from Alex's enticing
sister.

She would be a vine that grew and choked out all reason and restraint.

He *knew* this, deep in his bones.

He breathed in the cold air, hoping it would somehow
cool him. But he stood, shirtless and vibrating, heated
all the way through.

He heard a noise somewhere underneath the roar of
surf and wind. A kind of *squeak*. He looked toward where
he thought it might have come from.

And then there she was, illuminated in a warm cast of
light. As though his traitorous thoughts had conjured her,
there on the terrace down the way. It was not her room
she stepped out of. He did not know what room housed
those terrace doors, but not her bedroom, even though
she was dressed for bed.

Because she was far closer than a full house-length
away.

She wore a robe, but it was open, revealing a brief,
silky nightgown. The breeze fluttered over the fabrics.

He knew it was silk because he'd had to handle procuring her wardrobe himself. He'd handled every inch of
her life these past few months himself. Because no one
but him could know she was here.

And he *liked* it. He had been avoiding accepting that
realization, but he could not push it away in this moment.

He liked being her only point of contact. He *liked* being
her savior, and he damn well *liked* the way she looked
at him.

Even when he shouldn't. What did that make him? No better than the controlling, abusive men in her life thus far. She deserved better than that, but he did not know how to give it to her.

He saw her mouth move but could not hear what she said over the sound of ocean and wind and storm. When he shook his head in signal he could not hear her, she held up a finger, then disappeared.

The storm outside echoed in him. It was not a good-night gesture. It was a *hold on* gesture.

And he had nothing to hold on to when he heard the door behind him open. He turned slowly to watch her enter his bedroom. She moved through the room, her robe still open, the nightgown brief and flirting with her golden thighs. Her feet were bare, her hair down and wild around her shoulders.

She looked more nymph or siren or something from some old painting. Dangerous, seductive, a cautionary tale. He knew all the cautions, wanted to heed them, and yet…

"What are you doing up?" she asked conversationally as she went to stand next to him on the balcony.

Her robe was still undone, and the nightgown she wore dipped low, offering a tantalizing glimpse at the perfection of the tops of her breasts. She would be soft, fragrant and responsive, because while he didn't think she was here for seduction *alone*, she knew what she was doing.

What she was after.

He forced himself to look away from the sweet, golden temptation of her skin and stared out at the ocean, focusing on her words, not her intent. What was he doing up? Wondering how he'd gotten himself into this mess where she became the sole center of all his thoughts, wants, desires.

Like he was eighteen years old. Obsessed, and righteous with it. A woman's sole protector from those who would hurt her. It *should* be noble, until a man used it as an excuse to hurt. To be violent himself. To follow that violence to its natural conclusion.

As Gabriel once had, to *almost* disastrous results.

But he could not verbalize this to Evelyne.

She sighed, an awed, satisfied kind of sound. "Isn't it beautiful?" she murmured, leaning against the railing. "I never knew how much I would love living next to the ocean, especially since it's hardly some tropical paradise, but it's better somehow than sun and blue. It's moody. Brooding. I think I even enjoy the cold." She smiled up at him, a goddess among mortals. "You made an excellent choice."

The curve of her mouth beckoned him. Lush and soft. The wind tangled in her hair, fluttering a scent of florals and sea around him like some kind of potion meant to tempt him. She would be a dream come to life if he pressed his mouth to hers.

She would be his end if he did not extricate himself from *this*.

"I have to leave," he told her, the words coming from some strange place of panic he didn't recognize. He had never panicked. He had plotted, he had acted. He had been in some…dangerous situations here and there for his job when dealing with people who were not altogether on the up and up.

Never once had he panicked.

But he recognized this need and its potential to turn

him into what he'd been at eighteen. Obsessive, vengeful and *wrong*. No better than King Enzo with his manipulations and violence.

"Why?" she asked.

"I've been called away to work."

"Have you?" she murmured, her mouth curved into a smile.

Like she didn't believe him. Like she saw through him.

When certainly neither should be nor *could* be true.

He pushed off the balcony and moved back into his room. Never in his life had he *lied* to a woman about his reasons for leaving, probably because never in his life had he had to *run* from a woman. In any other situation, he would be sure he was made of sterner stuff.

But she tempted him, and she was the one temptation he could not allow. The one temptation that could never surface.

He found his bag—thankfully mostly packed—and tossed it on the bed. "I should be gone closer to a month this time." Perhaps longer, but he didn't need to say that. He put his laptop that sat on the desk into his bag. He'd leave his toiletries—there was nothing in the bathroom he could not replace once safely home in Milan. Perhaps he'd go to his other estate in Sydney. Surely that was as far away from Maine as he could be. He would find a woman. He would remind himself that what had taken over his mind was simply temporary.

That he was stronger than it.

He made a move to shoulder his bag, then realized somewhat belatedly that he was not wearing a shirt. Yes, he would need a shirt. And shoes. He set the bag down, but there was a problem.

Both shirt and shoes were on the other side of *her*, unless he crawled over his own bed.

He would not *crawl*.

So he stood there.

She stood in his way. Purposefully, he knew.

Her gaze roamed his face, like a tentative, explorative caress. He should have stopped it, sidestepped her. Instead, he stood frozen as she moved closer, gracefully, a bit like a ghost. A ghost that haunted, that played with his mind, because he did not move out of her reach.

He held himself perfectly still as she reached up, with those slim, elegant, princess hands to touch his face. Her fingertips danced across his cheeks. Her eyes were luminescent, her lips pink and lush. She studied his face like it was a marvel.

"Gabriel," she murmured, his name shaped by her lips causing a bolt of lust to obliterate the recriminations he tried to hold on to. "You do not need to leave. I do not want you to leave."

She moved to her toes. He reached out to stop her, to push her back down on her heels, to move her out of his way so he could walk around her.

Instead, his hands found purchase on her hips and stayed there, the soft fabric a whispered promise against his palms. *Her skin would feel even better.*

Perhaps that thought, and the attempt to fight it, distracted him, because it gave her the chance to brush her lips across his. The low beat of need held him in his grip. It was shame that he had not had the fortitude to stop this before he had been given a chance to linger.

But linger he did, in this half-kiss. Gentle, almost nothing pressure, even as his grip on her hips tightened, bringing her up closer, plastered against him. He could feel the weight of her breasts, the shuddery intake of breath. The way his own body turned to painful, hardened *need*.

She smelled like something fresh and new. Spring and promise. It would haunt him the rest of his life, he had no doubt. And if he got a taste of her...

No, it would be a step too far. A step he could not take back.

So he had to put a stop to it. Now. He set her back on her heels, ignored the ringing in his ears, that pulling, incessant need that he knew too well led him to dangerous places.

He focused all his energy on making sure his voice sounded like a scolding schoolteacher, though his breath felt ragged in his lungs. "That was uncalled for, Evelyne."

"Uncalled for," she echoed. Her color was high, her golden eyes dreamy, her hands on his shoulders. The scent of her, the faint taste of her lingered, fogging up his brain for a moment before he had the good sense to step back, away from her grip on him.

She touched her fingers to her lips, still looking at him. He had a very disconcerting *upended* feeling. For most of his life—even when he'd been traveling down the wrong path—he had always felt in control. It wasn't loss of *control*. It was letting base urges win. He would have succeeded in murdering that man, if Alexandre had not waded in and pulled him off. If Alex had not said the words that got through the haze of violence and revenge.

You are not like my father, Gabriel. I will not let you fall down that path.

So he had never once let himself follow the path of obsession again. These days, he remained one step ahead of anyone who might lure him below that surface. He was intelligent, privileged and quick.

But he was not one step ahead of her. Not even close. If he'd listened to his instincts instead of believing he had a handle on the situation, he would have been gone long before now.

So he had to use whatever tools he had to stop this. Now. Cruelty seemed the only way, much as he loathed to treat her badly. It was for the best. "A little hero worship is natural."

She held his gaze, not getting haughty or even narrowing her eyes at him as he'd expected. As he'd *hoped*. Instead, she *smiled*. "Then why won't you let me worship?"

That had more than just his throat tightening. He could not find his voice for a throbbing, portentous moment. When he did find it, the sound was rough, pained. "Evelyne, I do not know what you think is happening…"

"Well, apparently nothing is happening. Though I don't see why." She gestured at him. "You aren't…uninterested."

Uninterested. If only he could even conjure the meaning of the word in this moment.

"Do you remember what you told me that night I broke you out of the palace?" he demanded.

Her eyebrows drew together, as if thinking back and coming up empty.

"You told me, in that haughty princess way of yours, that your brother would kill me if I took advantage of you." And he did not believe this exactly—because Alexandre was good and right and had once stopped *him* from killing a man—but there were dungeons in Alis, among other punishments.

She reached out, slid her palms up his chest before he stepped away. "You wouldn't be taking advantage. Have I not made that clear?"

He caught her hands by her wrists. Slim, her pulse skittering under the weight of his fingers.

For a moment, he forgot himself. He thought only of the feel of her hands against his skin. And he held them in his own. He could put her hands exactly where he pleased. He could...

"You're bored," he said, forcing his voice to be commanding and cold. Forcing himself to believe the words he said. "You're lonely. I'm not your plaything."

She looked up at him, head cocked, the gold of her eyes glowing like a hypnotist's pendant. "Why not?"

He thought he should be outraged by how flippant she was being. Instead, he was aroused. Tempted. If she wanted to play...

"I'm not a virgin, you know," she continued, turning her hands in his grip so that her fingers trailed along the underside of his jaw. "I can be your plaything right back. Perhaps I am lonely and bored. What would be so wrong with...entertaining each other?"

Entertaining each other. It brought to mind a million scenarios, but he did not let his mind settle on one. He thought of another time, when the obsessive want for a woman had obliterated all else. And his only savior had been...

"Your brother."

"Is a continent away," she said, as if every excuse of his was *nothing*.

He could not let himself be fooled. But by God he

wanted to be. The *want* of it all beat in him, loud and tight as any drum.

"I cannot contact him," she continued, her gaze watching where her fingers touched his jaw. "And he cannot contact me. If you feel so certain he would be…disapproving, he would not have to know. No one, in fact, would have to know." Her gaze met his. Direct. Seductive. "But us."

For a moment, his grip tightened. For a moment, he thought giving in was all he had in him.

But this was Evelyne, and he had promised to save her. Truly save her. Not sink her into his darkness like he once had another young woman. Not become a monster like the father he'd saved Evelyne from.

You are a monster, Gabriel. That old voice. That old reminder.

Yes, he could be. But he would not be.

He dropped her hands and whirled away, furious with how she had somehow turned all his normal protections on their head. "Have you thrown yourself at anyone who shows you a modicum of attention?" he demanded of her.

He knew how to be mean. He knew how to cut an unwanted pass off at the source. He knew how to accomplish all these things. To keep that surface level. To never allow anything deeper.

For her *own good*.

Why didn't they seem to work on her?

No one would have to know. But us.

He found his shirt, jerked it on. Everything inside him was a hard, tense ball. "I'll be back in a month or so."

"It was about a month just five minutes ago. Now it is a month *or so*?"

He shouldered his bag, gave her a cold look. "Behave, Evelyne." He moved past her, almost to the door.

"Run away, then."

He stopped, midstride, turned in utter shock. "What did you say?"

"I said, *run away, then*," she replied, enunciating each word carefully. A bright, glittering challenge. She even lifted her chin.

He moved for her then, swift and furious, and held himself back with his last shred of strength. He towered over her, desperate to put his mouth on her neck where her pulse fluttered. On her breasts, right where he could see the outline of her hardened nipples through the fabric of her nightgown.

Instead, he kept his voice cool and cutting. "If I fell for your sad attempts at seduction, it would be *you* who would be wanting to run away. Except it would be too late for you. You're a sheltered, pampered *child,* and you know nothing of the real world, or a *man's* wants."

She didn't drop her gaze. Color didn't even bloom on her cheeks. She raised a regal eyebrow.

"You forget, Gabriel, where I grew up. I may be lacking in education, the ability to cook or take care of myself in a country under a fake name. Perhaps you are even right about a *man's wants* and how little I know of them, but I know how to handle angry men. I know what *really* drives them, and you aren't angry at me."

"No?"

"You're angry at yourself, because you want me too."

He stood there, breathing through the truth. There was no way to win this fight. He recognized that, just as Alex had once taught him that sometimes you could not advance, advance, advance. Sometimes you had to have the wherewithal to separate from your feelings and retreat.

"Goodbye, *principessa*," he said, and then he left her. Not sure he'd ever return.

CHAPTER SIX

EVELYNE CLUNG TO the belief that Gabriel would return, did not allow the fear he wouldn't to take root.

Perhaps he wished to never have her throw herself at him again, but he wouldn't leave her without a way to survive. If he was so worried about what Alexandre would think about *seduction*, then he'd certainly be too indebted to Alex to leave her to fend for herself *forever*.

And more… He was too good of a man to let that be how he abandoned her. He had brought her here because of Alex, but he had not sat at dinners with her, listened to her, had actual conversations with her for *Alex*. He had not procured her paint and such for the house for *Alex*. That had been for *her*.

There was something more between them than just her brother, than just him saving her.

She told herself that for three long weeks. Long weeks where she spent an inordinate amount of time thinking about that night. About the way his mouth had shaped to hers. Brief, far too brief, but he *had* kissed her back. His grip on her wrists had done more in a few seconds than grappling with Jordi in the dark completely naked had *ever* done.

Which had given her some pause, as she recounted the

moments over these weeks. Maybe she *was* a child. She thought not being a virgin meant something, but everything in that kiss, those few, minor touches with Gabriel in his bedroom had been something...far different than what *she'd* experienced.

It was like a whole dark, promising world she didn't fully know about.

But wanted to. And he had not been unmoved. She was not *imagining* anything. She had felt his want throb between them—in his gaze, in his anger. And when she'd told him that he was only angry at himself for wanting her, she had hit the mark. She *knew* it.

He had been cold and cutting, but she had seen underneath that. Just like she'd said—she knew all about angry men.

Besides, he hadn't really given a good reason for nothing to happen between them. He'd never said: *Evelyne, I do not want you*. No, he had brought up her brother, made snide remarks about her.

But he had not denied that an interesting and complicated heat erupted between them.

Sometimes, she touched herself and thought of him, and she was quite determined if—no, *when*—he returned, she would tell him so. Watch his reaction. She could picture it. He would get that pinched look about his mouth, but his nostrils would flare, his eyes would heat and his hands would curl into fists as if he could fight away his attraction to her.

She smiled to herself, because he couldn't. He wouldn't have run away if he could.

Almost exactly a month after their kiss, three months into her life here on the Maine coast, Gabriel returned.

For the first time, he did not wait until nightfall. He appeared at the front door one late dreary afternoon. He carried enough bags that excitement and joy twined with troublesome hope so that her heart actually trembled.

Did he intend to stay for some time? Was it possible she wouldn't be quite so lonely anymore? Was it possible he had dealt with whatever…reservations he might have about her to want to explore this thing between them?

"What is all this?" she asked as he carried it all inside and dropped the bags and one box on the floor in the sitting room. She had repainted this room, switched out some of the furniture. It still wasn't perfect, but with one entire wall a window out to the sea, she was determined to keep working at it until she was satisfied. So she could sit in here and enjoy the beauty of the world outside.

"Supplies," he said, the word clipped. "We will go through them, and I will put them where you'd like, but I only have a few hours."

She blinked, some of her hope deflating, though a seed of it stubbornly held on. Surely he didn't mean… "A few hours?"

"I have a plane to catch at three."

This made no sense. He was here with all these things, and he was leaving in a few hours? On a plane? "To where?"

He did not answer her question. Instead, he opened one of the bags he'd brought. "These are contacts that will change the color of your eyes. The instructions for how to wear them are on the box, or I'm sure you can find some instructional videos to help learn if that's necessary."

"Change the color of my eyes, but…why?"

"If you dye your hair as I've suggested multiple times, wear these color contacts and dress to hide your figure, you may enter society here. You will use the fake name and backstory I gave you. You should be able to take care of yourself just fine without these risky visits. I have brought you a car. You can drive, can't you? I have obtained you an American license that no one will be able to question."

It fully dawned on her. This was not a visit. This was not going back to the way things were or moving forward on a new path. Together. "You're leaving me," she said as he crushed all that horrible hope, causing a river of pain. "For good."

He did not look at her. He looked at all he'd brought. His words were formal and final. "It is for the best."

She would never see him again. She would never see anyone she knew again, or at least until she was very old. She would be wholly alone in this world for so long as her father drew breath. Tears filled her eyes, but she blinked them back out of habit.

She looked at him, refusing to meet her gaze. No. Just...*no*. She would not let him cast her off. Not easily. "Who's best?"

He still didn't look at her. "You *can* drive, can't you? I thought I remembered Alexandre making sure of it," he asked again instead.

"Yes, I can drive," she retorted, irritation and panic mounting in equal measure. "Though I suppose I haven't done it on the side of the road that they do here."

"You'll pick it up. Town isn't far."

Town isn't far. This was beyond anything she had considered, and her brain was struggling to catch up. She had spent the past month alone and now he was cutting off what little joy, what little connection she had.

All her hope. Again.

"What if… What if something happens?"

"Should you have an emergency, you can of course still contact me, but I cannot continue to live my life if I am continually popping in to keep you going every few weeks. I have work, Evelyne. A life."

"Other women?" she demanded, and didn't care if she sounded a bit like a harpy. She wanted to harp.

He gave her a sharp, disapproving look. *Finally.* "There are not *other women.* There are women. Because the word *other* suggests there is a woman in my life. And there is not. You are like…a ward. At best."

"At best." She laughed, bitterly she knew. *There are women.* Oh, she wanted to *hurt* him. She shook with rage, and she was self-aware enough to know underneath the rage was fear, but she was so tired of being afraid.

"All the boxes and bags are labeled. It should be everything you need. You have a driver's license, a passport, credit cards. Everything you could possibly need to be Lina Marino."

She tried so hard to fight back the tears, to focus on the anger, but this was so gutting. She had survived these past three months on his visits. And maybe she had been in some denial. Denial that this would be forever.

Now he was describing a forever in which she couldn't even be *herself.* She had to pretend to be some Italian billionaire's wife. Not even *this* Italian billionaire's wife.

She was free from abuse, but not *free.* She was utterly alone, and she could not even be herself. When he was here was the only time she could even begin to experience what *herself* meant. How would she discover who she really was now?

The first tear fell, and she quickly dashed it away with the back of her hand. "Is this really necessary?" she croaked out. "Couldn't you have just made me promise not to kiss you?"

He got very stiff then. "This isn't about that."

Fury leaped at that, twining in with the sadness, disappointment and fear. She looked up at him now, eyes narrowed. She settled on the fury, held on to it, nurtured it. She wanted *that* above tears. She wanted to *hurt* him as he was hurting her.

Fair? No. But none of this was *fair*. And if it wasn't, if nothing could be, if even in escape she could not have any sort of freedom, then why be fair? Or rational? Or anything other than *furious*?

"No, Gabriel, you do not get to pretend. You are punishing me because I had the *audacity* to suggest we might enjoy each other."

"It is not punishment," he returned flatly. But she saw something in his eyes. A kind of softening. Which did not make her feel better. It somehow made her madder. That he could be soft, that he could be *interested*, that he could be so many things when it came to her and want to cut them all off.

"I am not *punishing* you, Evelyne," he said with that infuriating gentleness.

"You are. You're leaving me *alone*. Forever."

Gabriel thought he could fight anything. He'd *prepared* to fight anything, even a bit of hysteria, but the tear that tracked down her cheek sorely tested that preparedness. Because it wasn't hysteria. There was a bone-deep sadness in her, even underneath this new flash of temper.

She had been cut off from all she knew, and he was her only anchor. But he could not safely continue to be this for her. She might be upset, but he was doing her a favor.

If she got under the surface any deeper than she already was, he would only make her miserable. He would only be shades of her father. Even if he never laid a hand on *her*, he would not be the man she thought.

He could not be the man she needed. Calm, rational, in control.

"If you wear the disguise, you can meet people. Make friends. Make a life here." He tried to keep his voice from softening. "It will not be so bad."

"But it will all be a lie." She dashed another tear off her cheek, but another spilled over and she left it there to trail down the soft gold of her skin. "No one will really know me. I cannot ever be *me*."

He could not let that truth change his course. "It was never permanent, Evelyne. Me visiting you. You must make your own life."

She shook her head. "Of course. What I want has never mattered. Why would I think that would start now simply because you saved me from marrying the general? It's all the same to the likes of you."

"The likes of *me*?" He thought of everything he'd done for her—not just Alex, but for *her*. Frustration wound deep with a nagging guilt that irritated him. He had nothing to be guilty for. Not when it came to *her*. He was doing this *for* her, so he would *not* be the *likes of* anyone who'd hurt her. "I would suggest you don't lump me in with your *likes of*, if they include your father and the general."

"Why not? Rich, powerful men who see women as nothing but pawns. Move me about the country. Leave me alone. Cut me off from everything I know—for my own good. Yes, I know. And I am grateful. But when do I get to choose for once? I didn't even choose this damn house."

"Leave it then. Find a new one. Do something else, if you want to be a child throwing a tantrum."

Her eyes widened then, got a little wild. He surveyed her warily.

"Would you like to see a tantrum?" she asked very quietly. The kind of quiet that was never safe for anyone. "I think I *will* throw a tantrum. I've never been allowed. If I cried, I was sent to the kitchens. If I yelled, I was beaten until I apologized. If I rebelled…" She shook her head. The tears didn't just *trickle* now, they poured out.

But she didn't sob. No, there was as much anger as hurt in her expression and her tears.

And it was too easy to imagine what she spoke of. King Enzo's fists and her delicate build. If anything tested his resolve, it was that. "Evelyne."

She whirled away from him, kicked over the box. The contents clattered around, but didn't spill out. That clearly didn't satisfy her, so she gave it another kick. When that did little more than clatter around again, she marched over to a little decorative shelf—new since the last time he'd been here. On it she'd arranged some colorful bits of shells and glass and tiny vases. She picked one of the vases up, hurled it across the room, where it crashed against the wall, glass splintering.

"How is that for childish?" she demanded. "Perhaps

now that you're leaving me alone, I will just *always* act like a child. Perhaps now that you're abandoning me after I was forced to leave everything I've ever known, *that* is what I will lean into. Perhaps *childish* is who I am, Gabriel."

Her breath was heaving, her eyes wide and wild. He wanted to find himself disparaging of her behavior, but it was hard not to understand. Yes, he had saved her—something he accepted knowing he'd enjoyed it too much, knowing the dangers of *saving*, but it's not like being removed from a threat and being plunked down in the middle of luxury meant she couldn't be *angry* that choice and hope had been stripped from her.

He had known she could be mad, but he'd assumed she'd handle it with icy, royal dignity. Some pithy remarks. *Maybe* he'd anticipated some tears. But not this wild, immature undoing.

Certainly not his reaction to it. Fascinated, aroused. She was usually so poised. Even when they'd been sneaking out of Alis, hopping from plane to train and back again, she'd kept up that regal princess-like behavior, wilted—yes, but held together. Even when she'd come to his room in her skimpy nightgown, tempting him, attempting to seduce him, she had maintained her control.

Now it was gone. She was the ocean, crashing against the rocks, furious and glorious all at once.

She grabbed another tiny vase, hurled it against the wall again. This one did not shatter, but it dented the wall, fell to the floor with a *thud*. "You get to choose to leave me. You get to choose to reject me. What do I get to choose? Nothing. Not even you."

He watched her eyes track to the last vase, and then the

giant window. "But if you're abandoning me, you have no say in what I choose." She said this with an almost eerie kind of calm after the outburst directly before it.

She reached for that vase, her eyes on the window. He wasn't sure it would do damage against the thick glass, but he wasn't about to let her find out. He crossed the room and took her by the arms. He gave her a gentle shake.

"Enough," he ordered, but he kept his grip on her arms so she could not fight him or try to destroy more. "Stop this now."

She tossed her hair back, chin darted up to stare him down, even though she was nearly a foot shorter than him.

"What are you going to do if I don't stop? Beat me?" she demanded.

But touching her was such a curse. He could think of nothing but the kiss they'd shared. The way she felt against his body. He couldn't even fully absorb her words, because he was lost in the golden threads in her eyes.

Even amid this wild tempest her scent was something sweet and delicate. For a month that scent had been at the edges of his life. There had been times he'd find himself distracted by it, look around whatever room he was in expecting to see her.

"You haunt me." He said the words as if he'd been cracked open and they'd simply fallen out. Against his will. Against his everything.

Some of that fury in her expression faded, but the chin didn't go down, the tension in her muscles didn't relax. She held his gaze, defiant. "Good."

Good, she said. *Good* as if any of this was *good*.

He knew what he had to do. Release her. Walk out of

this house. Never, *ever* return no matter what Alexandre asked of him.

There was still a way out. Just disentangle himself. Walk right out the door. Resist this one more time and then he would never, ever allow this temptation in his life again.

She bent her arms, and he did not let her go, but he did not stop what she was doing. Which was reaching up to her shoulders and pulling the straps of her dress down. Nothing could happen if he did not let her arms go. The straps would be stuck. She could not make this happen.

He dropped his hands. The dress fell. There was nothing particularly alluring about the underwear she wore under it. Serviceable cotton, he supposed.

But there was *everything* alluring about the woman who stood before him. Her hair, glinting honey in the cascading afternoon light, wild around her shoulders. The pale golden expanse of her skin. She leaned back against the wall behind her as if in offering to him.

Even as his body raged with want, he catalogued every beautiful feature. He thought he could have spent his entire day just looking at her.

But Evelyne had other plans.

"Touch me." She reached out, took his hand. "Feel how much I want you."

Madness. Obsession. Danger that would obliterate everything he'd built. Some echoing voice in the back of his head told him to stop. This was the last step before stopping was not an option.

But he did not pull his hand away. He let her draw him to the apex of her thighs. He cupped her there, half convinced there was still some exit route behind this.

Her sigh, her gasp, the hot, needy heat of her as she moved against him, whimpering, proved that thought wrong.

And all exit routes were gone. There was only her. There was only this. He moved the flimsy underwear out of his way, teased her with his hand while the other tugged at the strap of her bra. All the while watching her eyes, the way they swam into nothing but golden heat. The way her lips parted, her breath panted, moaned.

He pulled the bra fabric away, then fixed his mouth to one tight nipple. She cried out, tensing around him, tangling her hands in his hair. Vibrating through the climax he felt ripple through her, while his body raged with unspent want.

She tugged his hair so he looked up at her. She met his gaze, her eyes cloudy with desire, but direct and fierce. So damn fierce. "I'm choosing this. You're choosing this. Take me, Gabriel. Before you leave me, my God, take me."

Whatever last grasp on control he had was obliterated. *Leave.* He had to leave, but by God, he had to have her first. Just as she said.

He jerked the bra all the way down, and she laughed in breathless excitement. He didn't bother to finesse her underwear off, just ripped it out of the way.

Then his mouth was on hers. Nothing holding him back. Only that desperate want that would be his undoing and his end. He tasted, devoured, glutted himself on the hot, delicious contours of her mouth.

She fumbled with his clothes, unbuttoning maybe two buttons before she just yanked, sending buttons flying. Then her small, slender hands were on his bare skin and he growled into her mouth, plunging his fingers into the wet, willing heat of her once more.

She moaned, wild and free. There was no timidity. Just giving. Just that same wild storm—heat and a loss of control and the desperate pull to destroy.

She would destroy him, he had no doubt, and with her body bared to him, golden and beautiful, he reveled in the destruction, in her. His hands roamed her body, tending to fires until she begged, pleaded, arched.

She worked to undo his pants, until he shoved her hands away and freed the painfully desperate erection himself. Then he lowered her onto the plush carpet beneath them, and in the same move entered the welcome heat of Evelyne. She came apart around him in one quick thrust, a glorious scream of pleasure as she pushed against him.

He gritted his teeth against the swamp of pleasure. Too much and not enough. He needed more. So much more. All.

All, all, all.

He moved inside her and she moved with him. She chanted his name, and she dug her fingers into his shoulders, demanding more. Demanding that *all*.

It was a storm. Perhaps it would destroy, but in the throes of it, Gabriel only felt the power, the pleasure. The rightness of plunging into her, again and again and again.

She moved against him, a wild, wanton mythical creature, too beautiful to believe she existed. She consumed him, until he felt like he was but a wave, crashing again and again against the rocky surf himself. Maybe they were nothing but wind and sea, crashing against each other, never meant to do anything but.

And he crashed into her one last time, a glorious release of everything. Disaster. Absolute glorious disaster.

When he could see again, he looked down at her. Her smile was smug and her eyes half closed, like she would just drift away into sleep, here on the living room floor in the middle of the afternoon.

But it was not over. It could not be over, because once it was…

He refused to think past that. He swept her up into his arms. He did not recognize what fueled him, what moved through him with her warm body tucked against his. It had a different tenor to everything he'd felt before, and yet he knew it was just as—if not more—destructive. It would be obsession, it would be vengeance, it would destroy.

In the moment, he wanted all that destruction. He carried her upstairs and all the way to her room. He laid her on her bed, and nothing about the smug satisfaction on her face changed him. She regarded him under dark lashes.

He stood on the side of the bed, rational thought trying to get its grip on him again. But she had other plans.

"Do you want to know what I did while you weren't here?" she asked him, sultry and full of promise, her intent whispering through his brain so that all the warnings went silent.

She lay naked on her bed, stretched out and magical. Maybe she was a witch casting a spell on him. The spell was better than anything he'd ever experienced.

"I touched myself and wished it was you."

His body hardened again, so easily, so powerfully. He *throbbed* with need. But he didn't touch. He didn't lower himself to her once more. He met her gaze. "Show me," he ordered.

Her mouth curved. "I dreamed of that too." She trailed one hand down her body, cupping her own breast with the other. She did everything to her own body he wanted to do with his own hands, but he watched instead, hardening as she brought herself to a glorious, crashing climax.

Her gaze met his as her breathing came in quick bursts. "You're better."

He had no response to that. To her. Nothing in words anyway.

He gripped her leg, pulled her to the edge of the bed, spread her legs wide so that he could see the glorious heart of her. He waited there, watched the color rise in her cheeks, spread over her breasts. And still he waited, drawing out the moment, the anticipation.

"Gabriel," she whispered finally.

And then he positioned himself at her entrance but then waited again. As she tried to move against him, wriggle closer. "I like watching you so desperate, *principessa*."

She huffed out a sound, frustration or amusement or both. "I would think you might like watching me come apart."

"That too. I like it all." He moved slowly. Drawing out the anticipation and pleasure. She was begging long before he was fully inside her, and even as his body demanded more, he stretched it out. Denied them both what they sought.

"Gabriel. Now." It was not an order. It was a plea. But she spread her arms wide, arched her body, taking him even deeper. "*Now*," she repeated.

And then something broke. Him. Both of them. Everything went wild and uncontrolled. Her screams, his demands, echoing through the house. The desperate sounds of bodies meeting. And her scent, still sweet and every-where.

He felt her fall over that sensual cliff over and over again before he could no longer deny himself. He emptied himself into her on a primal growl of triumph.

Yes, this. Her, always her. His.

At some point, night had fallen, and they had dozed, sated and perhaps mind numbed by all they'd found in each other.

When he woke, it was pitch-black, and Evelyne was curled up next to him, fast asleep, like that was exactly where she belonged.

His heart cracked, but he had been down this road be-fore. Maybe it felt different, but it would be the same ob-session, the same madness. It would drive him to places he could not allow himself to go.

It would drive him to places she did not deserve to witness.

Didn't all of this prove it? He should have never crossed this line. It was a betrayal of what Alexandre had asked of him, and it was a betrayal of all the promises he'd made to himself when he'd gotten his life back.

Even as need tried to find its way into his bloodstream once more at the feel of her warm body pressed to his, he felt cold. He could see it all clearly now. He slipped out of bed. She didn't stir.

Had he known this would happen all along? Had he *hoped* this would happen all along? He watched her sleep-ing form and accepted that, yes, if he'd truly wanted to stop this—he would have never returned after that kiss. He would have handled all of this from afar.

But he'd returned. He'd needed to see her one last time.

More though, he'd wanted just this. Her. And because he was weak, he had taken it. A mistake, but a fixable one.

He left her sleeping.

With no plans to ever return.

Evelyne had awoken to night outside her window and the unsurprising truth that Gabriel was gone.

Truly gone. He had left her. She knew he would not come back now. There was no doubt in her mind. Whatever he had allowed between them he viewed as an unfixable mistake. The heat, the passion, the glorious pleasure of it all was wrong in his mind. For whatever reason.

Evelyne sighed. She didn't cry then—tears would come later as she sought to live someone else's life. As she came to certain realizations. In this moment, she made a promise to herself.

She would make the best of what came next. She would live as Lina Marino. She *would* drive to town and make friends and build a life. Maybe it would be a lie, but it would be *her* lie.

So a few months later, when it finally occurred to her that the lethargy, the nausea, the tears that finally did come and didn't want to stop was a sign that she might be pregnant, she did not ring the emergency number Gabriel had given her. She did not contact him.

She calmly put the color-changing contacts in—though she refused to dye her hair—and drove herself to the store in town, purchased a pregnancy test, figured out the self-checkout so no one in the village she'd come to know would see and took it home.

When the test was positive, she still did not call Gabriel.

No, he had left her. And this was no emergency. This was her life, and she got to live it as she saw fit.

So she would do this on her own.

CHAPTER SEVEN

GABRIEL DID NOT go back. He was proud of himself for that. Because there were a few times over the course of the next six months that he had gotten close to breaking. Once, he'd even arranged for a plane.

He would have gotten on it, with no clear intention but to see her again, get his hands on her again, but he'd received an email from Alexandre that day about some party in Alis he wanted Gabriel to attend.

Gabriel had canceled the plane immediately, gone to the insufferable party and thought of Evelyne the whole time.

But he knew what would happen if he ever went back to her. He would not be able to resist. Because separation had not dulled this obsession. He thought of her, dreamed of her, cursed her.

Wanted her with every breath, like she had become the very air he needed to survive. It was insanity, this warped thing inside him. Because he could think of nothing, feel nothing, want nothing but her.

He would not allow it to tear him apart a second time. Perhaps it felt different from before. He thought more of *her* than avenging her.

But at its heart it was the same, so what did it matter?

When his phone rang one night as he tried to convince himself to go out, find a woman, he saw the screen read *Alexandre* and he answered it, teeth gritted. He felt an immeasurable guilt every time he spoke to his friend that did not go away with time or separation from Evelyne.

"Alex."

"You must come at once," Alexandre said with no preamble. "And I cannot explain until you get here."

So, quite against his will, Gabriel flew to Alis that very night, because Alexandre had not sounded himself, and it worried Gabriel. He arrived in the dead of night, and it was Alex himself who let him into the palace.

The prince *never* answered the palace doors.

"What is it?" Gabriel demanded on a hushed whisper—the dark, silent halls around them seemed to demand it. Everything felt wrong, but Alex vibrated with a strange kind of energy.

He leaned in close. "My father is dead," he whispered.

Gabriel wasn't sure he understood the words. "I beg your pardon?"

"We have not made it public yet. The doctors thought they'd be able to save him at the eleventh hour, but he took his last breath right before I called you. I have much to do. A million arrangements to make." He raked a hand through his hair, an almost never seen movement of being overwhelmed from the pri—the *king*.

Because the old king was dead. Enzo was…dead. It felt impossible, but Gabriel knew he had to be more than shocked. Alexandre had called him for a reason. For help. He would jump to do whatever Alex required.

"What can I do?"

Alex turned to him as if he just remembered he'd been the one to call him here. "You must bring Evelyne home."

Ice slid through Gabriel's veins. Evelyne. Home. He had to clear his throat to speak. "I'll send for her."

"No. No, you must fetch her. This is delicate. I have taken the oath, but until the coronation happens, things are very complicated. Especially with the general. I want her here for the coronation, but I do not want it to be publicized. Not yet. You must go get her and bring her here without anyone in the palace knowing. Ensure she is safe. We will not make the announcement until she is here."

"Are you certain..." Gabriel wasn't sure what he meant to ask, so he only trailed off, not sure how to proceed.

Alex laughed. Not a joyful sound, but not a bitter one. Just a kind of wondering. "He just...keeled over in front of me after dinner."

Gabriel said nothing, let Alex talk. Clearly he needed to say it, accept it.

"He was talking to me, muttering about some slight handed to him by some diplomat. He was planning a war." Alexandre shook his head. "And then he put a hand to his head, complained of a headache and just...crumpled. The doctors believe it was a stroke." Alex looked around the darkened entryway as if seeing it for the first time. "He is truly dead, Gabriel. I saw it for myself. A stroke."

"A stroke of luck, perhaps."

"I suppose," Alex agreed. He was looking into the dark shadows of the hall. His voice was very quiet, very tortured when he spoke. "He lay there, Gabriel, and I did not want to call for help."

"And why should you?" Gabriel returned, knowing his friend needed assurance, comfort, even as Gabriel's mind whirled with thoughts of Evelyne. "But you did call for help. There were doctors. So there is nothing to concern yourself over," he said fiercely, because he could see Alex doubting himself and it would not do.

One of them was a good person, and one of them was not. Alex would always be the good. Gabriel...never now.

"I suppose." Alexandre shook his head, as if to scatter unwanted thoughts. His gaze zeroed in on Gabriel again. "You must bring Evelyne safely home, Gabriel. As quickly as possible. I want my family together. To usher in a new era for Alis. A good one."

Good. God, Gabriel hoped so, but first he had to face Evelyne.

What he had done.

And would no doubt want to do again.

Evelyne was humming to herself as she turned into the drive. Her monthly appointment with Dr. Stevens had gone well. She liked the doctor, even if he was a bit elderly. He was sweet and kind and asked no probing questions about the missing father of her baby—unlike some of the nosier ladies at the general store who wondered aloud why they never saw her husband.

Dr. Stevens answered all her questions with a calm patience that soothed her. He was like a father—or perhaps grandfather—figure. And when he gave her advice, she listened. Like when he'd told her to stop reading about pregnancy online—her anxiety had calmed quite a bit since she'd done so.

She found she fit in better with the elderly population of Bay's Point. She did not know how to relate to people her own age, though she had tried. It wasn't just that she

was a princess, or had been raised so differently from
the younger people of town, it was that she was pregnant, and alone, and, probably since everyone thought
her incredibly wealthy, they viewed her as an oddity. Not
a potential friend.

But the older people of the town seemed hell-bent on
making sure she was hardly the oddest thing *they'd* ever
beheld, and there was a great comfort in that.

"Maybe I do not have any young friends yet," she said,
talking to her baby bump as she often did. "But we do
have *friends*, and they will be very helpful when you arrive, I have no doubt. You'll have better honorary grandparents than your actual grandfather, that is for certain.
And then, perhaps when you are in school, there will be
other children's parents to befriend. Maybe by then, I
won't be so odd."

It was a comforting thought, if a bit of a stretch. But
kindergarten in the States started at five. She could enroll
in a preschool before that. It *felt* a million years away, but
she was assured by anyone she talked to that the years
would fly by.

And she would have a baby. A child. "You will be
the light of my life," she murmured as she drove up the
winding drive to her house. There would be no cruelty.
No punishments. There would be only love.

She reminded herself of that any time she considered
calling Gabriel's emergency number. That her baby would
be wanted and loved and feel nothing but *joy*. Maybe Gabriel would not reject a baby as he had rejected *her*, but
Evelyne refused to take that chance.

Still, it left an ache in her heart. For him. For home.
For family.

"And maybe someday, when it is safe, I will be able to take you to Alis and show you your birthright."

She thought of her home, her brother. Would Ines be pregnant yet? The only reason for Alexandre to get married was to produce an heir. Would they have children around the same time and never know it?

She shook that depressing thought away. "Only happy thoughts," she told them both cheerfully.

But the attempt at cheer was immediately threatened by an unfamiliar car parked in her driveway and the worry that fluttered in her chest at all the possibilities.

But then she saw the man on her doorstep. He was not unfamiliar.

She sat in the driver's seat, simply staring at him. Maybe in those first few weeks she had allowed herself the tiniest seed of hope that Gabriel might return, but once she had come to accept she was pregnant, she had not allowed herself errant thoughts of his return.

She did not need him and his rejections, and neither did their baby.

But there he was. Looking as handsome as ever. Visions of their night together tried to take up residence in her brain, but she shoved them away. For many reasons, but the most important one was the child of theirs she was growing.

Some small part of her wanted to get out, dash to him, throw herself at him and tell him everything. Beg forgiveness. Beg him to love her, take her, care for them.

And that was so sad and desperate she stayed where she was. She had to figure out a way to get rid of him without him seeing. She didn't know what his reaction would be, and he'd *left*. Never checked in on her.

So his reaction did not matter.

But she could hardly just ignore him. He was *right there*, staring at her as he came down the stairs and toward her car.

Handsome. So *stern*. She did not understand what about *her* brought out the stern and tortured in him when what appealed to her was his charm and light with everyone else.

Tentatively she rolled down her window. "I do not recall issuing you an invitation." He did not need to know about the gift he'd left her with.

Not until she knew why he was here anyway.

"We do not have time for childishness, Evelyne. Get out of the car. Pack a bag. You must come with me."

Childishness. So disdainful, so demanding. After the way he'd left her. "Why should I?" she returned archly.

He studied her face in return, and her heart trembled. He was so serious, and clearly here against his will. This was definitely not reconciliation, so it had to mean something was *wrong*. "Is it Alexandre? Is something wrong?"

"Alex is fine. It is your father. He suffered a stroke."

"A stroke." She couldn't imagine it. The hearty, powerful, untouchable King Enzo Lidia...suffering a stroke.

"He is dead, Evelyne." Gabriel moved closer to the car. "You may return home. For good."

Evelyne tried to absorb those words, but they refused to penetrate. Dead. Return home. Dead.

Dead. Her father, her own personal demon, was dead. Just...gone. In the blink of an eye. And she could go *home*.

"Get out of the car so we may have a real discussion," Gabriel ordered. "And get you back to Alis."

Home. Dead. It was all so much to wrap her head around, and he was right. She couldn't just sit in this car and wait for him to go away, even though she needed more time to figure this out.

He thought he would take her *home*.

She looked up at the beautiful house she'd tried to accept was hers forever. She had spent time forcing herself to think of this place as the place she would raise her child. And there *were* so many things she'd learned to like about this place, this house.

But particularly since becoming pregnant she had *ached* for home. For her brother. For the familiar. She *liked* her friends here, but it was not the same. She had known she couldn't go back, would never subject her child to an Alis ruled by King Enzo, so she'd tried to accept that.

But what about an Alis ruled by King Alexandre? It was almost unfathomable in all the positive possibility.

She looked at Gabriel, who studied her with his dark eyebrows drawn together. Perhaps she should refuse. Perhaps that was her only choice to keep her child a secret.

But why should she now if there was no King Enzo?

Because he *left you.*

Which felt a bit childish now that there was more at play. She had to figure out how to work through it somehow. Sitting in this car wasn't that. So she picked up her purse, her jacket. She tried to arrange them all in front of her so that she could hide the bump. It wasn't unwieldy just yet, but it was getting there.

Carefully, angling her body just so, she got out of the car. She didn't bother to look at Gabriel. "This feels like some kind of...trick."

"It is no trick. The king died yesterday. Alexandre has tasked me with bringing you back home before the announcement is made to the kingdom and then the world. He wants you at the coronation."

Coronation. "Alexandre will be king." She wasn't sure she'd ever be used to it, so sure it would not happen until they were both old themselves. "He will…" Tears filled her eyes. Not just hormones. A relief from a tension she hadn't known she carried. It fully hit her now, with Alex in charge, he would not be in danger from her father's vicious whims. With Alex in charge, everything changed. Decades before she'd thought that possible.

But in her emotion, her *elation* and relief, she didn't hold the bag and coat just as she should. She saw Gabriel's eyes widen. She tried to recover, but it was too late. He'd seen.

He pointed at her—at her stomach. "What is that?" Gabriel demanded.

She had dreamed of this in her weaker moments. Telling him that he was to be a father. In her fantasies, she was calm, casual, disdainful almost. She did not give him the satisfaction of thinking that she needed him, wanted him, or was afraid of being alone.

She was determined to make fantasy a reality.

So she beamed at him, made sure she sounded cheerful. "In the States they call it a baby bump." She ran her hands over the roundness, moved to give him a profile view. Refused to let the nerves fluttering through her show—she'd had ample practice at hiding those. "Isn't that cute?"

He said nothing. Didn't move. She wasn't sure he breathed.

When he finally moved, it was with clear-cut precision. "Explain yourself," he said quietly, dangerously.

She chose to maintain her flippancy. "Is it not self-explanatory, Gabriel? I am pregnant."

"By whom?"

She startled a bit at that. She'd *assumed* he'd jump to the natural conclusion. Did he really think she'd just…immediately hopped into some townsperson's bed after him?

It ached, almost as bad as him leaving her. That he'd think so little of her. She refused to even acknowledge the question. "I will need some time to pack." She started to walk up to the porch, but he caught up with her.

She expected him to take her by the arm, but he stood in front of her blocking her bodily. Like he was afraid to touch her.

She almost hoped he was.

He pointed at her stomach again. "Evelyne… Is that baby mine?"

He was so *good* at poking at her temper. She used her purse to slap him across the chest. "Of course it's yours, you asshole." And with that, she pushed past him and stormed inside.

CHAPTER EIGHT

GABRIEL STOOD IN a bright sunshiny end-of-summer day in Maine in *America*, winded.

Of course it's yours.

It couldn't be. None of this could *be*.

Not because it was impossible—in his lack of control he had not used protection, a fact he remembered all too clearly *now*. It was impossible because he did not know how to move forward. When he *always* knew how. He had made mistakes before, but none had cut him off at his knees leaving him reeling and absolutely uncertain how to…exist.

Even losing his control and sleeping with Evelyne had left him with a clear course of action. *Leave. Never return.*

He could not leave now. He could not take her back to Alis in her condition.

What had he done? And what the hell could be done *about* it?

Of course it's yours.

A child. A *child*. He had left her six months ago and she'd carried a *child*—his child—all this time and…

And not told him. She had kept this a secret from him. If the king had not died… She might never have told him.

A child would be alive, breathing, growing and he would not have known.

It was enough of a glimmer of something to *do* that he stormed inside after her. He found her in the kitchen, humming as she put together a sandwich. Happy as you please, and definitely not packing as she'd claimed.

"You had my contact information," he blurted out.

"I did," she agreed. She took a big bite of the sandwich, looked at him with a careless smile. "I chose not to use it."

He opened his mouth, surely to say something intelligent and cutting. All that came out was some kind of pained grunt.

"You left, Gabriel. You made your feelings clear. You wanted nothing to do with me."

"You is not the same as *our child*." He did not like those words, could not fully engage with *child*. He had to think of this as a problem to solve or he might be forced to...*feel*.

There was a moment she held herself *very* still. Whatever reaction she had to the somewhat insensitive words was hidden in that stillness. She carefully set the sandwich down on the plate in front of her.

"Our." She laughed—it wasn't bitter, but it wasn't happy. "*Our.* How would there be an *our* anything, when you won't even deal with me? You run away."

The characterization of what he'd done—when what he'd done was *save them both*—still grated. "The last time I checked, people who run away did not leave their *contact information*."

She had the gall to roll her eyes. "You made it clear you wanted nothing to do with me. I mean, aside from sex. You seemed to enjoy that quite a bit."

"As did you, *principessa*." Which was neither here nor there, and certainly not the *point*.

She made a low, satisfied kind of sound that went straight to his loins with an arrow sharp intensity.

"How did you plan to explain this?" he demanded, so as not to think about his physical reaction to her.

"I didn't," she returned. She sighed in a way that made it clear she had had *months* to deal with this while he had only had *minutes* so far. "I would have kept him a secret forever," she said, and clearly meant it. She settled a hand over her burgeoning belly with a gentleness that thundered through him in ways he couldn't parse.

But he could not even be hurt by her *forever* because...

"Him." She would have kept *him* a secret forever. A boy. A son. No... He couldn't...

She was quiet for a long moment, almost looking sad. "Yes. Congratulations, it's a boy." She lifted her chin, finding her haughty. "I will *not* be naming him after you."

Naming... A boy to be named. His boy. His *son*. All Gabriel seemed to hear now was a high-pitched whistle in his ears.

"Do you need a paper bag?" Evelyne asked. When he stared over at her in confusion, she shrugged. "I saw this funny old TV show where someone hyperventilated into a paper bag."

"I am not hyperventilating," he ground out.

"Close."

"Evelyne, this is a mist—"

"Do not finish that sentence," she said fiercely, skirting the counter and stalking toward him. "I will not have anything bad said about my child. *Ever*. He will be loved and treated with kindness. Always. And he will never,

ever, not *once* be made to feel as though he was a mistake. He will never be a mistake to me, no matter how you feel about it."

Gabriel wanted to tell her it was impossible to ensure a child was *always* treated with love and kindness, but she looked so fierce, with her arm curved around her belly. In a strange, blinding moment he knew she would be a good mother. She would protect the child—their child—in all the ways she had not been protected *and* all the ways she had.

And what would he be?

A father. He did not know how to wrap his head around this. His life had been nothing but skating the surface of anything so important as *fatherhood* since he'd been eighteen. Only Evelyne had taken him back under dangerous old waters.

The things he would do for her without a second thought, the violence he would enact throughout the world to keep her safe. Perhaps he would never turn it on her, on their child, but he had the potential to be an echo of King Enzo all the same. A *reminder*.

What would a child do to him? What would that kind of love and devotion create inside him?

It was terrifying. Overwhelming. He needed to somehow keep this…separate.

Why was she always overwhelming him when he had *learned* for years to fight against anything that might wave over him and crush him?

But he looked at her and felt endlessly crushed. Not just by this *child*.

How could she be more beautiful than when he'd left her? How could the obsession run so deep that cold turkey had not staved off this destructive need? She was *pregnant*, ripe with child, and he wanted to touch every inch of her, hear her pant his name again.

Which was no doubt incredibly inappropriate. Obsession and destructive need. He could not be destructive with a child's life at stake. He needed to focus on the practicalities. On what must be done.

Not *her*.

"I have a plane waiting, Evelyne. If there is anything you want or need, I will collect it for you. But we must hurry."

She cocked her head, studying him. He couldn't possibly read her mind. Didn't want to, at *all*.

"I can get my own things. Pregnancy is not fragility." But she did not make a move to get her things. She continued to study him and went back to eating her sandwich. When she finally spoke, the question was one that he was trying to avoid thinking about.

"What do you think Alexandre will say?"

Gabriel could not begin to guess. There would be no approval, no celebrations, certainly, even if he somehow fixed this so Alexandre did not know about the six-month abandonment. Alex would not *approve*.

So Gabriel had to find some way to ensure it. Practicalities. Legalities. He was good at both these things. They were part of his job. How could he use his expertise to make this all right?

The only way Alexandre would even begin to accept this were if certain…legalities were in place. It was not what Gabriel wanted, but he would have to make it work somehow.

Without destroying them all.

"If we take the personal out of it, you are the princess. A baby out of wedlock will be frowned upon," he said, knowing he sounded stiff and not being able to do anything about it. "Not just by Alexandre, but by the kingdom as a whole."

"Are you suggesting we marry, Gabriel?"

She said it like a joke.

It wasn't a joke. "I am not suggesting. I am stating that we will be married, Evelyne. Now, in fact. Before we return to Alis."

Evelyne stood stock-still, watching him as he moved into action. He disappeared and returned with a laptop bag. He pulled out the computer, sat at her kitchen table and began to...work.

Marry. Gabriel. She should be appalled, she knew. He wasn't marrying her out of anything but a sense of duty or whatever to Alexandre. He did not *like* her, and she needed to really accept that. She did not want her child growing up knowing his father did not like his mother. A forced marriage certainly wasn't going to make that fixable.

"Gabriel. Alis might be a bit old-fashioned and traditional, but perhaps this is an opportunity to usher in some modern ideas. Like, I don't know, not making each other miserable with a marriage neither of us want."

It was a lie. She did kind of want it. Because she liked *him*. But that was pathetic, and even if *she* didn't mind being a bit pathetic here and there, she now had a child to concern herself with.

She would not be pathetic for him. She would be strong

and right and true. She would be an example of love and… and goodness. No matter the effort it took.

Gabriel looked at her, eyebrow raised in cool disdain. "Do you really think the time around your brother's coronation is the time to introduce *modern* ideas? Particularly when you have an entire army moving from a war-hungry king to one who will promote peace, and well they all know it."

Fear gripped her. She'd thought the danger died with her father, but… "Do you think he's in danger?"

"No," Gabriel said, with a certainty that eased some of her concerns. "Alex knows how to handle things. I'm only saying, I will not be adding to the things he has to handle. Any more than I already have."

Right. Because she did not just get to go *home*. She had to bring home a complication. She rubbed the swell of her stomach, chewing on her bottom lip. Should she take her child back to Alis with all this hanging over them?

But she thought of Alexandre. Of the palace. Of *home*. Even if her father had made her childhood hell, there was so much she yearned for back in the place she'd been raised. She wanted her son to have family. She wanted her son to have…

She studied Gabriel. She had not allowed herself to consider him as a father. As *the* father. She had spent considerable time just focusing on her and the baby. What she had, not what she wanted.

Now he was here. He was taking her home. He was talking about *marriage*. And it wouldn't be the kind of marriage she wanted, she knew that, but what if…

She shook her head. No. She couldn't introduce fantasies she'd avoided for six months just because he was here.

She moved over to him though, peered over his shoulder at what he was working on.

It took her a while of watching him to fully understand what was happening. He was…working to forge some kind of marriage record.

For six months ago. As though they had married *first*. A legitimate child under law. She wrinkled her nose, trying to work through how she felt about it. An unnecessary lie—she would *never* allow her son to feel *illegitimate* just because of how he'd been conceived. But this was something that would make Alexandre's life easier. And probably her son's, if she was being realistic.

But there was something under the practicalities. The war of truth and best choices.

"Ah, so we are not *actually* getting married." She refused to sound disappointed. She was *amused*. Damn it.

"There may be no ceremony, the date might be fudged, but it will be *actually* for all intents and purposes," he replied, without looking up at her. "From here on out."

It wasn't romance at all, and still her heart fluttered. They would be married. *From here on out.* And what did that mean to him?

"We will be husband and wife to everyone who knows us," he said, returning to his all-important computer.

"Will you share my bed then?"

His fingers fumbled on the keys, but he did not look at her. "That is hardly a concern right now."

"It is one of my concerns."

"You have a one-track mind," he muttered, typing away again.

"No, it has many tracks, actually. Some more enjoyable than others. For instance, I like to wonder what he'll look like, or plan the nursery, rather than read, think or *imagine* labor." She shuddered at the thought. There were so many worries, and she'd had to step away from them or get lost in them.

But there was one inevitability. This baby would come out of her one way or another. And the bigger he got, the bigger she got, the more impossible and inevitable it seemed.

She thought she could endure that inevitable if she was home. If she had the familiar, without her father's overbearing evil.

She thought—and knew it was wrong to think it—if she had Gabriel by her side to be her husband and this child's father, she might endure it just fine. Even if he didn't love her or like her.

Haven't you had enough of that in your life?

But Gabriel, for all his faults, was not her father. He was not *cruel*. His dedication to Alexandre no doubt meant he would be dedicated to their child.

Didn't it?

"We have not discussed what kind of father you will be. You can forge whatever documents you wish, tell Alexandre we are married, but these are…small details. The most important thing is this child."

She wasn't sure his expression was one of hurt. No, it was more…arrested. "I have a very good father. A very good example to follow."

"That makes one of us. What made him good?"

Gabriel blinked as if he did not know what to do with the question. "I suppose… He was a good man, who balanced his own needs with the needs of his family's. I assume my parents love one another, but I think just as important, I never doubted my father's respect for my mother."

"So you will have to work on that then."

He regarded her with a mix of emotion in his gaze that she could not quite make out. It was serious, weighty, but she did not know what it *meant*.

"And he did not leave us in Alis to become a pawn of the king," Gabriel continued, without addressing her comment.

"The dead king," Evelyne said, because she was still having trouble believing it's true. "My father is dead and I am free."

He glanced at her then, specifically at her belly. "You're pregnant, not free."

She didn't wish to engage with that, so she wafted away from him. "So the plan is to waltz into the castle. Hello, Alexandre. Allow me to kiss the ring, Your Majesty. Oh, by the by, I married your best friend. Baby on the way." She patted her belly to emphasize.

Gabriel was scowling now. "If that's the way you want to characterize it."

She did, because it felt silly that way. Not scary. Would Alexandre be disappointed in her? Would this baby... It suddenly dawned on her, if she was going back that meant...

"Is there another royal baby on the way?" she asked Gabriel suddenly.

He regarded her with a puzzled frown. "Not that I've been told. Why?"

Evelyne chewed on her bottom lip, a new trickle of worry jittering through her. "Do you not know the Alis law about heirs?"

"You'll be shocked to know I have not studied the line of the Alis throne."

She had been given no choice and had never given it much thought because of course Alex would be first.

But he wasn't. "The firstborn of the king's children is the heir. It does not matter who the parent is. Alex will be king as long as he chooses, of course, but then…"

"You're saying our child will be the *heir*? That we have…usurped that from Alexandre's future child?"

"I do not think Alex will mind overmuch." She really didn't, but it felt good to say out loud. "I do not think being an heir served him enough to care about that. Though he might wish he hadn't capitulated to father and married. I quite like Ines, and maybe he does too, but it is certainly not love."

"She has made him a good wife. He has said so."

"Ah, romance *does* exist," she said sarcastically.

He did not engage with that. He closed his laptop and stood. "Now that we are married for all intents and purposes, it is time to go, Evelyne. It should all be settled by the time we land. If there is anything you want, I will send for it once we arrive in Alis. Alexandre will not relax until you are home, safe and sound."

"Even if I'm pregnant? And his best friend is the father? And, oh yes, we're married. Very relaxing thoughts."

"Perhaps relax is not the right word," Gabriel muttered. "But we must go anyway."

So Evelyne allowed herself to be led out to the car, away from the house she'd tried to make her own, tried to love. Away from the ocean and its comforting power.

And started the journey back home.

CHAPTER NINE

GABRIEL DID NOT believe in *anxiety*. He was not a man who allowed himself to worry. He dealt with. He acted.

But the tight band around his lungs as they drove up to the palace under the cloak of night was *something*, and he could not seem to work his way through it.

He felt Evelyne's hand curl over his, squeeze. He was horrified she might see the worry in him, but when he glanced over at her, he realized it was she who was worried. She watched the palace get closer with wide eyes and clear distress.

But when the car pulled to a stop at one of the private, side entrances, she let out a slow breath and smiled over at him.

"Thank you for bringing me home."

How could she undo him so simply? To thank him for something he wasn't even doing *for* her. He was doing it for Alexandre. If it had been up to him…

Gabriel said nothing and got out of the car, but he skirted the hood and made it to her door before she managed to open it. He did so, then braced himself for impact and offered his hand to help her out.

She took it, and he was grateful that in the dark he could not make out the expression on her face. Or he might be inclined to keep her hand in his. He might be inclined to hold her close and assure her everything would be okay. Instead, he broke the contact.

Except, it was dark out here, and he worried that in her condition she might trip over something or… Cursing his life choices, he tucked her arm into his so he could guide her. "I will come back and get our things later," he told her quietly. The door had been left unlocked for him, so he pushed it open and ushered her inside.

Much like when he'd arrived the night of the king's— the *former* king's—death, the palace was dark. Gabriel led Evelyne through the dark hall, keeping her arm in his, until they reached the king's wing.

Alex had instructed them to meet him in his private library, so that was where Gabriel lead Evelyne. The warmth of light from the doorway cascaded out into the hall, and Evelyne's pace increased when she saw it, their arms disconnecting.

Gabriel told himself it was relief that coursed through him. Certainly not regret.

She made it to the door before he did, and stopped there, taking in whatever sight was before her. Gabriel couldn't help but watch her face. The excitement, the joy, the relief, the *love*.

It roiled around inside him like a sickness, but he forced himself to continue forward. To step into the library with her.

Alex was pushing himself out of a chair. He set down the book he'd been reading, his eyes on Evelyne.

"Evelyne." Alexandre moved toward her with a genuine smile on his face. A rare thing for a very careful and private prince.

King, Gabriel corrected himself. Alexandre the *king*.

Evelyne's expression bloomed, and tears filled her eyes. She moved for him too. They embraced tightly, and said nothing, but the way they held on to each other spoke volumes.

Gabriel had understood that they worried about each other, but he had not realized perhaps how much that separation and worry for the other had weighed on each of them. How much they had simply missed each other. Though Alexandre had spent many years at boarding school with Gabriel, it was no doubt the siblings had long since relied on each other to be safe places in their father's awful kingdom.

They had both done some excellent acting over the past nine months to pretend as though the separation had not been as soul crushing as it had been for them.

It eased something inside Gabriel to see them together. To see them happy. A relief, his own version of joy, and feelings deep enough to cause him even more worry. This was not the surface level he needed to operate with.

Until Alexandre moved back from Evelyne with a frown on his face. He looked down, and while the coat she wore hid much of her shape, no doubt the tight hug gave away what lay beneath. "What…"

"Surprise," Evelyne said cheerfully. She shrugged out of the coat she'd been wearing that had somewhat hidden her baby bump. She turned to Gabriel and handed him the coat. The worry and nerves he'd seen in her eyes on the drive in were nowhere to be seen now. Gabriel knew it was an act, but it was a hell of an act.

"Evelyne…" Alex was shaking his head. "What…"

"I know it's a surprise, but I hope not an unhappy one."

She patted her belly. "I am happy, and I think that should be taken into account. I know how much you respect Gabriel. We only kept it a secret because of Father. And now he's gone, so now we don't have to. You're happy for us, aren't you?"

"Happy..." Alexandre's eyes moved from Evelyne's stomach to Gabriel. "You..."

Evelyne moved over to Gabriel, slid her arms around his waist, looked up at him lovingly.

An act, he reminded himself when the warmth of the gold in her eyes shuddered through him like a promise.

"Gabriel saved me. Not just from this place and the general, but my sanity when I was alone and homesick. He was so kind and understanding and...caring. Which, as you know, was in short supply around here."

"Evelyne, I don't understand," Alexandre said, moving his gaze from Gabriel to his sister.

But she kept chattering on, inventing this phony love story. "I've always had a kind of crush on him, but this allowed us time to really get to know one another as people, as adults, and why... I just couldn't help but fall for him." She patted Gabriel's chest, grinned at Alex as though everyone was just as happy as she was pretending to be. Instead of shell-shocked on his way to fury—which was what Gabriel thought Alex was.

"I'm sure you can't blame me for that. You know what a good man Gabriel is. And well, I happen to think I'm a bit of a catch myself," she quipped.

Gabriel could not bring himself to look at Alex. His gaze was caught on Evelyne's hand on his chest.

He needed to get her a ring. And since that felt like something blatant he should have thought of, his only option was to cover her hand on his chest with his own. Hide his failing until he had a reason for it.

"It wasn't that we wanted to get married without you. It was just...we wanted that commitment. That promise to one another." Evelyne beamed up at him. It was *almost* too much. *Almost* amusing. He *almost* found himself smiling back down at her. "We certainly couldn't wait—or thought we couldn't—for Father to die. So we married, and now we are expecting."

"Married. Expecting..." Alexandre said these words like he didn't quite understand the meaning of them.

"I'm sorry if that ruins your...procreation plans," Evelyne said, looking at Alexandre now. "It was not exactly planned. We got carried away on the wedding night... Well, you don't need to hear *that*. I only mean to say, I don't wish you to be angry with us."

"Of...of course not." Alexandre cleared his throat. "Surprised, but not angry. Perhaps without the pressure, Ines will... Never mind." He raked a hand through his hair, reminding Gabriel of the night King Enzo had died. "You must be exhausted," Alex finally said, his voice sounding a little rough. "We can... Let us get some sleep, deal with everything...in the morning."

"Alex..." Evelyne crossed to him then. Before she could say anything, Alex put his arm around her shoulders.

"I am happy for you, Evelyne. Very happy. It has just been...a lot of change in a short period of time. We will get through it, but I think it's best if we all get some sleep tonight."

Evelyne nodded. "All right. Yes. I'm...so happy you're

king now." Gabriel watched her swallow. *This* emotion was not put on, even if her story was.

Then her gaze tracked to his. "Gabriel has taken such good care of me."

Which was a *lie*. He had left her alone for six months. Pregnant. She held some blame for that—she *could* have told him. But he still felt the guilt sting.

"But I'm so happy to be home," she continued.

"A joy only equal to mine, Ev. Get some rest now. I… I should go tell Ines you are home." His eyes darted to her stomach, then to Gabriel. "We'll have a nice family breakfast in the morning. The…four of us."

Alex crossed the room to Gabriel before Evelyne moved. "Congratulations, brother." And Gabriel might have been fooled into believing there was an actual congratulations behind that, but Alex didn't stop there.

He spoke the rest quietly, possibly so that only Gabriel himself could hear. "We will talk in the morning. *Before* breakfast. Alone."

And he did not sound like a man talking to his friend. He sounded like a king ordering his subject.

Evelyne walked to her room in silence. She didn't know what to say, and it was so dark and quiet in the hallways. She was exhausted, and a little hungry. She didn't have the energy to ask for something to be sent up, but she did have some snacks in her purse.

She yawned as Gabriel opened her old bedroom door. How funny to have Gabriel in her old room. It felt like her previous life had belonged to a different person. The thought of poor, cowardly Jordi almost made her laugh.

Gabriel was a great many things, perhaps even a coward when it came to *her*, but she had no doubt he'd stand up to any threat for her and her child. He wouldn't run away or stand down to a threat. Even if he didn't love her.

He was here, wasn't he?

She stopped short a few steps into the room. Everything looked...exactly the same. She turned a slow circle. A picture of Alexandre and their mother still sat on her bureau. The linens on the bed were the same she'd picked out when she'd been sixteen—pink and frilly, befitting a princess. Everything in this room spoke of a life of ease and luxury and royalty.

She supposed that had been purposeful. Some of the staff knew how her father treated his children, but he also kept much of it under wraps. This had all just been a veneer over the horrible truth.

And still, she'd *loved* the pink, the ruffles, the picture of the mother she'd never known. Much of the decor didn't fit who she was anymore, but it still felt familiar and like home.

Home. Except with none of the old fears. Because her father was dead. Every shackle, every abuse she'd suffered here was just gone.

Evelyne did not know how to fully absorb it just yet.

"What is wrong?" Gabriel asked when she just stood there.

"Nothing." Evelyne blinked back some tears, no doubt aided by the hormonal parade going on inside her. "I just assumed... I assumed Father might wipe any sign of me out, but everything is still here. Untouched, almost."

"No doubt Alexandre's doing."

"No doubt," she agreed, finally moving forward. Alexandre. She thought she'd done a pretty good job of

smoothing over a lot of unexpected information, but…
"He didn't seem happy," she murmured, wandering over
to the cushioned window seat. Though it was dark outside, she could picture the gardens in her mind.

"Did you expect him to be?"

"I suppose not."

"He was happy to see you, Evelyne."

She inhaled deeply. Yes. Perhaps he'd been a little off-
kilter, but there *had* been so many changes, and he was
no doubt bearing the brunt of them. Well, now that she
was back perhaps she could take on some responsibility,
ease some of his.

She turned to face Gabriel. To deal with the fact it
wasn't just her same old room, it wasn't just Alex, Gabriel
was in her life now. Permanently, more or less.

She studied his expression. Guarded. Stiff. He didn't
want to be here, but he was. What did she do with that?

A childhood of abuse, coupled with a brother who did
everything he could to protect her from what parts of the
abuse he knew about, had taught her that her only option
was to roll with the punches.

She thought she'd done a pretty good job, through the
past nine months of her escape and exile. And something
about this pregnancy had supported the one truth she'd
held on to to get her through the tough times.

Yes, there were *always* tough times, things to endure.
But there was also always goodness and hope and something lovely on the horizon. Life was peaks and valleys
of good and bad—sometimes all at the same time.

So it was imperative to reach out and relish in the good,
hold on to it while it was there. She could be offended by

Gabriel, she could be mad at him, she could bemoan the fact he didn't love her.

Or she could just enjoy him. Take what good there was in this situation and let that outweigh the bad.

She studied the handsome man in her bedroom, who she was now technically married to even though they'd said no vows. Perhaps that was not *good* as a whole, but there were parts of good to be found within this situation.

"I suppose you will have to share a bed with me, whether you want to or not," Evelyne said, trying for innocent, no doubt sounding smug. "If you want Alex to believe my little story."

"And what a story it was," he muttered. He ripped his tie off and tossed it on the chair. Frustration was at a boiling point, she could tell. And perhaps it was her great tragedy that she *liked* his boiling point. She *loved* when he lost control.

It was like seeing under a very shiny surface. Oh, she'd enjoyed his smiles and charm. The innate ease of friendliness he'd moved about the palace with *before*, but seeing the explosions underneath had revealed a much more interesting and alluring man.

Or you're just really messed up.

He undid the top button of his shirt like he was feeling a bit…strangled.

"Let me help," she said, moving over to him. She reached up to the second button and undid it before he grabbed her wrists and stopped her forward progress.

"We will not be doing this again," he told her darkly, stepping away from her and letting her wrists go.

She sighed. Would she always be throwing herself at him? Maybe. And maybe she should find some sort of shame over that, but for all her exhaustion, there was something else winding its way through her body, and she wanted him to take care of it.

Six months she had done her level best not to think of him, what he'd brought out in her, what they'd brought out in each other. But he was here now.

She smoothed her hands up his chest, just as she had done the first time she'd thrown herself at him. Would it ever get old? Would it ever start to be embarrassing?

Or was the sex just *that* good?

For both of them. Whatever his reservations about her, they were not their physical compatibility.

She still remembered the exact growled tenor of when he'd said she *haunted* him.

Had he thought of her in such ways these past six months? She hoped it tortured him, the thought of their night together.

But not enough to withhold the same now.

"Why not? We are married. You said so yourself. We are *actually* married and will function as such. I will not tolerate affairs, so I suppose you shall have to settle for me if you're expecting to enjoy more than your hand."

He scowled at her, but she saw the sparks of heat. Of want. Whatever he thought of her as a person, there was no denying they had chemistry.

A good. A good she wanted to enjoy.

"If you're worried about the baby, it is perfectly safe. Every book I read said so with annoying clarity." She moved to him again, this time putting her palms on his chest like she had the first time she'd kissed him. "Like a constant reminder I *could* be having sex with you and wasn't. Because you weren't there."

He looked down at her, his expression stoic and unmoved. But his body wasn't.

"What do you think is happening here?" he demanded.

"We are married. I like the way you make me feel. I like *you*. I don't know why you hate me so much, but I know you enjoy my body."

His scowl deepened, if that was even possible. "I do not hate you."

"You do a marvelous impression of dislike then."

"Dislike." He said the word with such disdain. "If only I disliked you, Evelyne."

She cocked her head. He sounded so *tortured* and she didn't understand. "I think if you liked me, you wouldn't be so dismayed to find yourself here." And still she moved her hands up his chest, around his neck, pressing her body against him—though that was quite a different experience with a baby bump between them.

"It must be nice to have such a simplistic view of things. Like. Dislike. Black. White."

She wondered if it was a flaw in herself that she found his disdain so funny. "All right. I have a simplistic view, what with this simplistic life I've been given." She gestured around her. She didn't need sarcasm to do the hefty lifting here. The palace itself would have been a complication even if her father had been given a heart.

Nothing was ever simplistic, but maybe that's why she did not get hung up in the complexities. They simply were.

"What is your complex view of the situation, Gabriel? Enlighten me."

"You are a smart, vibrant young woman." She thought he made a kind of move to remove her arms from his neck, but it was almost like he was afraid to touch her, even though she was touching him. "Your resourceful-ness has been incredibly impressive. You're even funny, when you aren't trying to torture me. I have no reason to dislike you. Except for the torture, I suppose."

I have no reason to dislike you. It wasn't poetry, and yet she felt her poor romantic heart softening. He'd called her impressive. "Then why do you *behave* as though you dislike me?"

"Have you ever considered something darker and far more volatile?" he demanded. "Has it ever occurred to you that my obsession with you is unhealthy and that your insistence we act on it makes an already difficult situa-tion untenable?"

He sounded so—the word he used—tortured. It made very little sense to her, but she liked the explanation. If it were true.

"You're obsessed with me?" She eyed him critically. She didn't know how leaving her for six months was ob-session, but if that's what he claimed…maybe she'd claim it as well. "Though a six-month disappearance doesn't quite support that theory, I rather like the idea."

He shook his head as if despairing of her. "You won't," he said darkly.

"Perhaps I should be the one to judge." She moved to her toes, managed to angle herself enough to press her mouth to his. She wanted obsession. That all-encom-passing need and pleasure she'd found in his arms back in Maine.

She wanted *him*. Here in her old life that would soon become her new life. With him and their baby. So *many* complexities. But what else was new?

He kissed her back in spite of himself, she knew. That

it was physical reaction, not choice. Because he kept his hands off her, like he thought he could avoid this if he only kept his hands away from her body.

She pulled her mouth from his, scowled at him. "Oh, touch me, Gabriel. It is what we both want."

As if he'd been waiting for a command—and God knew he was not waiting to be told what to do, since he *couldn't* be told what to do—the leash on all he held back broke.

His hands were reverent, and it send waves of warmth and need through her. It was different, because her body was different. Because they were married. Because they were home. Because nothing had actually been settled, but he couldn't run away this time.

She wouldn't let him. Alex wouldn't let him, and actually, she didn't think he'd let himself. He would feel too responsible for the baby she carried now that he knew about his existence.

And so while the tensions he tightened inside her were the same, it was not the storm crashing between them. It was not anger and fear, and maybe that word he used—obsession. It was something deeper.

They were in it now. No way out. So they sank into the ocean that took them over. Onto the pretty pink bed, ridding each other of their clothes, until they were skin to skin, body to body.

His mouth tasted, his hands tormented in all the best ways. His body was a thing of glory—muscled and masculine. She roamed him with her hands, with her mouth, as he returned the favor.

When he moved her on top of him, seated deep inside, she looked down at him and felt like the ocean herself. A powerful, undulating storm that would not be satisfied until she'd crashed to shore over and over and over again.

And his gaze, stark and hungry, a powerful magnet. She moved against him, and they watched each other as the tension grew, coiled, and hers…exploded. He sat up, holding her in his lap, still deep inside her, and pushed her up, up, up again. Closer and closer to one more shuddering release.

She held on to him, whispered his name, reveled in the physical glory. She bit his shoulder, and he growled as his grip tightened, as his body tightened and then thrust one last time, pulling her down tight on top of him so that she catapulted one last time into that vibrating ocean of pleasure he always gave her.

Life was not simple, no, but it was so simple to give herself over to him, to enjoy him, to be with him just like this.

And when he did not immediately lecture her or get out of her bed, she smiled and curled into him. Perhaps he did not want to be.

But he was hers now. She cuddled in closer, rested one hand over her belly.

Theirs.

CHAPTER TEN

GABRIEL WAS NOT surprised to be summoned to Alexandre's office before the sun was up the next morning. He was already out of bed, watching Evelyne sleep, when the tap at the door came.

He could not come to grips with his next steps. So much of what she said made sense—they enjoyed each other, they were married, she was already pregnant, why not have sex? Why not share this bed and this room and behave in all the ways a married couple expecting their first child should?

But he knew the answer. Because he could not trust himself. The darkness of this obsession would only sink deeper and deeper until it damaged *something*. He didn't know what yet, but it didn't matter. The fact she even threatened the surface way he'd moved through life proved to him he could not be trusted.

But there was a child now. An undeniable fact. Staying away from her was not the answer, but what the hell was?

He had to find a way to…fix it. But he had time. He had three months to figure out how to navigate this before their child arrived. That was his deadline.

He would never remind her of her father. He would

never give his child a reason to fear. There had to be some alternative.

When Gabriel walked into Alexandre's office, he found him seated behind the desk waiting for him. He had not taken over King Enzo's gilt, over-the-top office, but had instead continued to use his own. Minimalist and stark, no doubt in direct response to his father.

Still, this was not a welcoming environment. Gabriel was not surprised there was no evidence of any place for him to sit.

This was to be an interrogation. One he undoubtedly deserved.

"Good morning, Your Majesty." Gabriel greeted Alexandre with as much royal reverence as a man who did not particularly believe in kings could manage, even for his best friend.

Alex did not return the greeting. "Please explain to me how you have come to be secretly married to my sister. How she is *with child*, and how I clearly would not have been privy to either piece of information if my father had not died unexpectedly and I demanded you bring her home."

Gabriel had to work not to scowl, because it reminded him that *he* would also not have known if not for that. And blame or anger or hurt had no place inside him if he was to make the appropriate plans for Evelyne and their child.

"Perhaps we should toast to Enzo's gift to us?"

"Answer me, Gabriel."

Gabriel didn't sigh, though he wanted to. He stood, hands clasped behind his back, searching for some explanation that was the truth because he did not wish to lie to Alexandre. But there were certain lies that must be told.

"Evelyne and I..." He struggled against the need to rub his hands over his face. *Evelyne and I.* Parents. Married. "She is an intelligent, witty, beautiful woman, and while I certainly didn't expect to...be so taken with her, it became undeniable."

"She may be all those things, but you took her away at my bequest—young, alone in a strange place, bereft, and dependent wholly on you."

Because those things were all technically correct, except maybe the bereft part, and yet didn't take into account the *scope* of Evelyne and all she was capable of, Gabriel stiffened. "I do not take advantage of women, if that's what you're accusing me of. I would never take advantage of Evelyne. Perhaps she is stronger than you give her credit for."

"You do not take advantage of women, agreed, but ever since..." Alexandre let the silence stretch out between them. Long and meaningful. Meant to be heavy and perhaps even a little cruel. A reminder of Gia, and what he'd been willing to do to save her.

Gabriel could not deny he deserved the stark reminder.

"You have not been serious about anyone since then," Alexandre continued. "I'm not sure you've been serious about anything, except maybe your work and even then, there's a certain casualness to your success there. And now you have married and impregnated my sister, two very serious and permanent steps. You can understand my concern."

"Yes, I can. It...was not planned. It came as a surprise, these...feelings for her." He sought to find some fine line of truth inside the lie, sought to not wince at the word *feelings*. He had to walk this line, between convincing Alexandre he could handle this without diving into obsession and violence, but that he was also not *flippant* about the situation, or Evelyne. "I tried to maintain a certain superficial distance, but it became impossible. She is…unique. It pains me not to give her what she wishes." Truth enough.

"And what do you wish, Gabriel?"

Hell if he knew. But he met Alex's hard gaze. "I shall endeavor to make them both happy."

"Endeavor," Alexandre scoffed. "Such a bland word."

"What would you prefer?"

"Ensure."

"Very well, I will ensure they are both happy." He did not know how he could possibly ensure such a thing, but he supposed he had no choice now.

Alexandre narrowed his eyes, studied Gabriel with that quiet, stoic intensity he had employed even as a boy. Like he'd been born with such abilities. Born to be a king.

"You are my best friend. I respect the man you have built yourself into. And while I know *you* do, I do not hold your youthful indiscretions and Gia's influence against you. We all have crises of self and fate, particularly at eighteen. It is not the crises that define us, but the choices we make in the face of them."

Gabriel felt as though he was a young man getting a lecture from a much older person. Perhaps his own father. Someone he'd *also* have to tell about this, but he wasn't ready to consider his parents just yet.

"My sister is now the mother of the future monarch. Your life will change. You did not know that going in. You thought, like I did I would imagine, that my father would hold on to life and the crown for quite some time. But these facts change things."

"I am aware."

"Are you?" Alexandre replied, quite royally. He stood now but stayed behind his desk. "You will be given a title. We will have a royal wedding ceremony of some sort. Your child will be the future king or queen of Alis."

It was...too much. Too many things to fully engage with. He wanted none of those things, but he could hardly deny them. The child existed. He would be an heir. *He* would be... "Future king. It is...a boy."

"A boy," Alex repeated.

And they stood there staring at each other, that fact between them, both perhaps feeling like they were children again, wondering how the years had zoomed ahead to the point where they were the ones *having* children.

"Evelyne has not had an easy life. I know on the surface it is all privilege, but surely you understand just how...ugly things have been for her."

"Yes." Gabriel gave Alexandre the only truth he had in him now. "I will do everything in my power to shield her from all the ugly from here on out."

Even if the ugly was him.

Evelyne was starving when she woke up. When she glanced at the clock, she couldn't be surprised Gabriel was not in bed. She'd nearly slept the morning away.

"All the books say to enjoy that now," she said, running a hand over her stomach. "That you will be keeping me up at all hours of every night soon enough. You wouldn't do that to me, my darling, would you?"

She got out of bed and moved into the closet. She

frowned at her options. Since she hadn't had a chance to pack her maternity clothes, she only had items that suited a much thinner and different woman.

"What I have back in Maine will be suitable sometimes, but I will need an entirely new maternity wardrobe for royal events and the like, if your Uncle Alexandre has any plans to announce my marriage and pregnancy to the public."

She smiled at the idea of *Uncle Alex* as she found a pair of soft, stretchy pants that were a bit tight as such, but she rolled the waistband down under her stomach. What had once been a dress now fit like a somewhat odd tunic. She studied herself in the mirror, chuckled in spite of herself.

"Not very princessly, I must say."

"Who are you talking to?"

She glanced up at Gabriel. She hadn't heard him come in, and now he stood in the entrance to her closet. "The baby."

He looked dubiously at her stomach.

"You should give it a try."

He did not respond to that invitation. "Alexandre has requested our attendance at lunch since you slept through breakfast."

"Good. I'm starving."

She slipped on the sneakers she'd worn yesterday, which made her clothes look even more ridiculous. Then followed Gabriel out into the hall. She tucked her arm into his. He stiffened, though he didn't pull away.

"Are you afraid you'll lose all control and take me on the table in front of my brother and sister-in-law if we touch arms on the way?" she asked him lightly.

"You are such a comedian, Evelyne."

She laughed in spite of herself at the disgusted note to his tone, but then she was distracted by her surroundings. She came to a stop in the hall, stood there for a moment, absorbing all the details that remained the same despite her father's absence in the light of day.

"Is everything all right?"

She looked up at Gabriel. "Yes. Better than. I was just thinking how it's all the same even without Father here, and yet...it *feels* different. Lighter. Like I can breathe."

"Strange how a lack of threats of beatings might allow a person to breathe."

Before she could decide how to respond to that, she heard her name being called. She turned and saw Ines bustling toward them.

Ines smiled brightly at her and greeted her with a light kiss on Evelyne's cheek. "It is so good to have you back. My world has been *very* masculine since you left." She held Evelyne at arm's length. "And look how pretty you are. Glowing."

"I don't know about all that. The wardrobe certainly leaves something to be desired."

"Excuse me, ladies. I have a quick call to make. I'll meet you in the dining room."

They nodded as Gabriel took his exit and the women tucked their arms into each other's as they walked down the hall to the dining room.

"I told Alexandre already, but I did want to apologize. It never occurred to me that... Well, I wasn't thinking about heirs and such. Especially all the way over in America. It was not my intention to take this from you and Alex."

"Of course not," Ines soothed.

"I'm sure Alexandre could change the law!" She grabbed on to Ines's arm, because the truth of that occurred to her. "Oh, that's it! It's so hard to believe he's king now, but since he is, he can change anything he wishes. He can certainly make your future baby the heir instead."

Ines smiled tightly and said nothing, which made Evelyne realize she was being…horribly insensitive. Alexandre and Ines had been married for nine months now, and there was no discussion of a pregnancy.

"I'm sorry. I…" She shook her head, squeezed Ines's arm. "I've read so many different women's accounts, it should have dawned on me that it might not be… That this may be a delicate subject for you. I'm so sorry, Ines. Tell me to shut up."

Ines shook her head. "You have nothing to apologize for. According to the doctors, everything is fine. No fertility issues, for either of us. It simply hasn't happened yet. They've encouraged us to be patient. Alexandre and I have not discussed it yet, but for me, I do not care if our child…should we have one, is heir or not. I know it is why Alexandre married me. To have an heir." Ines swallowed, but though she was friendly toward her sister-in-law there was a careful wall between them. They were not real friends.

Evelyne hoped someday they could be.

"Everything will be just fine." Ines patted her arm and led her into the dining room. "Alexandre will handle it as always. You don't need to worry at all. Now, let's eat."

Alexandre was already there, and they exchanged pleasantries, sitting down. Gabriel came in as the food was being put out. The conversation was superficial, friendly and *weird*.

Evelyne kept expecting her father to come storming in. Any time the door opened—whether it be someone to bring in more food, take away dishes, or bring Alex a message—she flinched.

She hoped it wasn't noticeable, but knew it was when Gabriel put a hand on her leg. He would not offer comfort unless she was very obviously doing a bad job.

"I suppose we must have some formal ceremony for Father," Alexandre said as the meal wound down.

"Must we?" Evelyne muttered, earning a bit of a chuckle from Ines. When Alex gave them both a cool, kingly glare, they sobered.

"Why not tell the truth?" Evelyne suggested. "He was an awful man, and we do not mourn him, and they shouldn't either. They've lived under his reign. I'm not sure anyone would be surprised to find their war-mongering king a violent and vicious man everyone is glad is dead."

"What does the truth get us, Evelyne? I am afraid all it does is make us look complicit. Which isn't wrong, but I'd rather not advertise it."

"It *is* wrong. What were we supposed to do? Foment a bloody coup?"

"Instead, we did not rock the boat and people suffered. It is not so simple."

There was that word again. *Simple*. No, nothing was simple. People had suffered. *She* and Alex had suffered. Suffering seemed to be the theme.

She glanced at Ines and Alexandre. They did not look at each other, regard each other, or seem to connect in any way. Did they suffer too, in this marriage they had not wanted?

The thought depressed her.

"Perhaps we can do a three for one. Coronation-funeral-royal wedding ceremony," Evelyne said on a hefty sigh.

Alex *tried* to keep his frown in place. She *watched* his lip twitch ever so slightly though. She'd amused him in spite of himself.

And that's how she knew she was finally, really home.

CHAPTER ELEVEN

GABRIEL HAD NEVER minded a royal event before, but he'd never had to attend one as *part* of the royal family. In the past, he'd shown up as a guest, which required almost nothing from him.

Now he was involved in a flurry of events, meetings, debriefings, fittings, plans. Because he was to be an *earl*. Gabriel tried not to be bitter about such things. If he'd wanted to steer clear of royalty, perhaps he should have kept his pants on.

First, Alexandre had announced the king's passing and Evelyne's return. He let the people draw their own conclusions about that and enacted a small, private funeral that was photographed for the Alis papers. No videos were permitted. No public ceremonies were planned.

None of the former king's citizens protested, though there was some grumbling from the general and his army. Gabriel did not know what Alexandre did to handle it, but it was handled.

And then coronation arrangements went into full force. The planning was giving Gabriel a headache, and he could only take so many work calls to get himself out of fittings and meetings to go over protocol. Because it wasn't just Alexandre's coronation. The marriage and Evelyne's pregnancy would be announced and then Gabriel would also be given his title.

It was to be a day of looking forward to a positive future, so Alexandre and Evelyne said. Gabriel felt mostly dread. With his parents due to arrive tonight, the festivities beginning tomorrow, he did not know what else to feel.

This was not the life he'd planned—which only reinforced the strange notion he hadn't *really* had a plan. Work. Be successful. Skate through life without following into the depths of rage and obsession that might otherwise grip him.

Was that a life? He didn't like to think too hard on that question that lingered.

After ducking out of a protocol meeting to deal with some work, he tried to escape to Evelyne's room, hoping she would be off with her own meetings and fittings.

But when he strode in, he found she was having a fitting right here. Someone had set up mirrors and one of those awful platforms, and two women were bustling about Evelyne dressed in her royal finery. They pinned this, tutted over that, made notes on little pads of paper.

But Gabriel simply stood and watched her. She looked so regal and at ease. A princess through and through. That tight fist of need centered in his solar plexus. He didn't know how to fight it. Days and nights with her only seemed to make the band tighter and tighter.

Her gaze met his in the mirror. Her mouth curved like she could read his thoughts, and they pleased her. Did she not understand the ticking time bomb inside him?

"We'll make these last-minute adjustments, ma'am," one of the women said as the others began to tidy.

"Thank you, Joan." The other woman helped her out of the dress. It looked like it must weigh as much as armor. Gabriel frowned a bit, wondering if he should intervene. She should be off her feet more, not worried about these frilly royal events. One of the attendants helped Evelyne into a robe, and she finally stepped off the platform.

Once finished, the women gave him little bows as they left the room.

Gabriel nodded at them, but his gaze stayed on Evelyne. She belted the robe above the swell of their child.

"Are you hiding from your protocol meeting?" she asked, her smile amused rather than disapproving.

"I do not hide, Evelyne."

"Of course not," she agreed, making him want to smile.

He resisted. "Are you sure you should be putting yourself through all of this?"

"I feel fine," she returned. "I always enjoyed this part of royal life. I know it sounds silly, but when Father was alive, I liked to think of it as a symbol. If I looked royal, then behaved as kindly and charitably to everyone I met, it meant that even though *he* wasn't those things, there was some hope. For anyone who looked at me and saw those things." She sighed heavily, looking away from her reflection in the mirror. "Perhaps Alexandre was right, and we were just complicit, and I like wearing fancy dresses."

She didn't look miserable exactly, but he could see just how Alexandre's words at lunch the other day had disturbed her. Gabriel knew Alexandre carried ridiculous weights on his shoulders that weren't his, but he hadn't expected such from Evelyne.

"It's far more complicated than that, as I think you

know," he told her with some force. "Complicit victims are still victims."

She looked up at him, a smile on her face. "I'm glad you think so."

When she looked at him like that, a hint of vulnerability in her happiness, he wanted to say a million things that would cause her to look at him just so. Like he was always her savior.

"I don't like to think of myself as a victim though. Look around, Gabriel. It was hardly a hardship."

"Your father beat you."

She inhaled, held it there for a moment. "Well. Yes."

"Did you think you deserved it?" he demanded, because the thought she might not know it was just wrong, simply wrong, and no amount of *amenities* made up for it, filled him with a rage he had no outlet for.

The king was already dead.

"Well, no. I mean…"

"Can you imagine laying a hand to…our child?" He tried to avoid discussing the baby too much, interacting with the idea of a child too much. Whatever securities he could implement to keep himself detached, surface level.

She met his gaze, searching for something. He turned away before she answered.

"No," she said quietly.

"Then that is all you need to know." He stared out the window, wished it was the Maine house with the terrace doors and cold whipping wind outside. He'd go stand there and watch the storm and be stilled.

He felt her come to stand next to him. He didn't dare look at her.

"I suppose your parents never…"

"No. Not once. It never occurred to me that they might. My father's disappointment held much more weight than any threat he might have given me."

She tucked her arm into his, leaned her temple against his biceps. "I am excited to meet them. I'm so happy our child might have one decent set of grandparents."

They would be that. Gabriel hadn't spoken to them much. They were overjoyed—not so much at the royal side of things, but that he'd met a nice woman and settled down—their words.

They did not know about Gia, about what was inside him. They did not know obsession could turn to violence. That every step of loving Evelyne and their child was a chance he'd become his own version of King Enzo and his parade of destruction.

So they only saw the positive. Gabriel was glad for it, but it made him dread their arrival more than look forward to it as he might have otherwise.

Gabriel left her, but his words, his assurances didn't. It was a comfort that he didn't try to undermine the abuse. Alexandre didn't do it on purpose, but sometimes she thought since he considered it *his* due, he considered it hers as well.

Which wasn't fair. Alex had protected her and spared her as much as he could. She knew one of the weights on his shoulders was that he had not done *more*, but sometimes it felt like he thought of her like…another country he had failed.

Rather than a sister he had done his level best to protect.

She sighed a little wistfully. Perhaps she could convince Gabriel to have the same talk with Alexandre that he'd just had with her. Perhaps Gabriel could get through to him and allow him to realize that no amount of abuse was their *due*.

She patted her stomach. "And that, my sweet baby, is just the kind of man your father is. For all his faults."

She should start getting ready for dinner. She was eager to meet Gabriel's parents, as he spoke so highly of them, but she was tired and achy and procrastinating.

When the room phone rang, she thought about ignoring it, but guilt and responsibility were too much to ignore it. "Hello."

"Your Highness, Mrs. Marti has requested an audience before dinner. I have her in your sitting room, but I can tell her you are not ready for visitors if you prefer."

Evelyne sat up in her bed. Gabriel's mother wanted an audience *before* dinner. Without Gabriel? Nerves danced around her chest. But she could hardly say *no*. "I'll…be there momentarily."

She moved out of bed quickly. Luckily she'd already picked out the dress she'd wear for dinner. Since tomorrow would be full of formality, it was far simpler. And comfortable. She hurried through getting dressed and took enough time to brush out her hair and make up her face a bit.

Once ready, nerves battling around inside her, Evelyne forced herself to enter her sitting room. She was a princess. She was incredibly used to walking into meetings with people she didn't know what to expect from.

But she had never wanted to impress someone so much

as she wanted to impress Gabriel's mother. She couldn't help but think that would go a long way in…something.

When she entered, Mrs. Marti stood and curtseyed prettily, making Evelyne feel a bit awkward even though she'd been curtseyed to often in her life.

"Sorry to keep you waiting," Evelyne offered, plastering a tight smile on her face and walking over to Gabriel's mother. She was a small woman, trim, her dress a beautiful plum that surely made her look younger than she was.

"A pregnant woman never need apologize for that." She crossed to Evelyne. Took her hands. Her smile was wide and welcoming, and there was an array of emotions in her expression Evelyne couldn't all parse, but she recognized them as happy ones.

"He has your eyes," Evelyne blurted out, then felt heat creep up her cheeks. What a silly thing to say.

But Mrs. Marti beamed. "Yes. My eyes and temper. Hopefully the baby will escape the temper part." Before Evelyne could think about *temper* and *Gabriel*, his mother continued. "You are looking lovely, Your Highness. You probably do not remember when we met before."

"I'm sorry. I didn't realize we had."

"It was the last time my husband and I visited Alis, before we decided to not return ever again. You were only three or four. And pretty as a picture, as you are now." Mrs. Marti squeezed her hands then began to bustle her to the couch. All the while talking.

"I didn't want our first meeting to be some formal royal affair. I know Alexandre means well, but he is just a man and cannot understand such things sometimes."

Evelyne smiled in spite of herself as she was nudged into a sitting position. "Yes, he is just a man."

Mrs. Marti laughed and sat next to Evelyne. "I wanted just a few moments to meet the man my son married without telling me."

"We are sorry."

"I understand that things with King Enzo were…complicated. I can't hold it against you, as much as I might like to." She smiled though, like she really did understand. Then she picked up a small package from the table. "I brought this for you."

"Oh…"

"For *you*. Not a baby gift, though I will shower my grandson as well when he arrives, but I always thought the woman carrying the child never got enough attention."

Evelyne felt overwhelmed with too many emotions to name. She didn't know what else to do but open the gift when Mrs. Marti urged her to.

The box was small, the beautiful pendant inside delicate and stunning. And it reminded Evelyne of Gabriel's eyes.

"You're a princess so no doubt you have access to the most beautiful jewelry, but this is an heirloom. It has been passed down in my family for many generations."

"Mrs. Marti—"

"Bianca."

"Bianca… I couldn't possibly—"

"Gabriel is my only son. My only child. I had always planned to present this to his wife once he married—unless I hated her."

Evelyne looked up at the woman, a little desperate to

have this connection but not feeling like she deserved it. "You don't know me."

"I know Alexandre. I knew your mother. And I know my son. I won't hate you, Evelyne."

Evelyne's breath caught. "You knew my mother. I suppose I knew that, but I didn't realize…"

Bianca smiled sadly. "I'm not sure I knew her *well*, but we were friends as much as anyone can be friends with a queen. Manuel brought me to Alis after we were married. The king had not fully ended Alis's relationship with Italy yet, so Manuel was still working as a diplomat. Your mother and I were pregnant at the same time, so she would invite me to teas and such."

"Alexandre always says she was…perfect."

Bianca laughed. "No one is perfect, though I'm sure she was perfect to Alex. Poor boy. She was very good. Very, very kind. Too soft for the likes of this place." Bianca's smile went sad at the edges. "She would have loved you very much."

Tears filled Evelyne's eyes. She swallowed at the lump in her throat. She didn't have the words. She didn't have… anything. *She would have loved you very much* would stick with her for all her days.

"And since she is not here, *I* will be. Manuel and I have a life in Italy, but now that King Enzo is gone, there is no reason to fear coming back to Alis whenever it is wished. We will be at your beck and call, I promise." She patted Evelyne's stomach. "And his."

"Mrs.… Bianca… I…" She flicked a tear off her cheek. "I'm overwhelmed."

"You've had so much thrust at you, and so quickly. Of course you are." Bianca scooted closer, put her arm around Evelyne and squeezed. "And growing a little one is hard work—physically *and* emotionally. It's a study in overwhelm, but you'll handle it beautifully. I have faith in the woman my boy chose."

Chose. Not really, but Evelyne could hardly lay that at Bianca's feet. So she changed the subject. She pulled the necklace out of the box, fastened it around her neck. "How does it look?"

"Beautiful." Bianca beamed, her own eyes a little wet. "You're such a beauty, it's no wonder you caught Gabriel's eye, but you have your mother's kindness. It shines through you."

Evelyne didn't know what to say to that. It put a lump in her throat she couldn't speak around. She had this angelic idea of her mother, thanks to Alexandre, and even though Bianca did not consider her *perfect*, to hear a nice account, and that Evelyne might take after the woman she'd never met… It was just too much.

"I have worried about my Gabriel, you know. He used to be so driven as a young man. He and the prince so…full of determination and plans. Something happened when Gabriel was younger, I do not know what. I have never been able to understand, but he changed. Not at his heart, thank goodness, but just in how he moved through the world. Such a…lack of direction. Oh, he was successful, that business of his. Good at it, for certain."

Evelyne wondered if whatever happened was what Gabriel had referred to Alexandre saving him from. Whatever darkness might have ended him. What might have happened to Gabriel that even his mother did not know about? That would have changed him so deeply?

Would he ever tell her? It was hard to imagine a situation where he let her in that intimately. He was always holding himself just a little bit back. Claiming obsession and acting… She didn't know.

"But he lacked an…anchor, I suppose," Bianca continued. "He does a wonderful impression of a man who knows what he's after, but I'm his mother. I can see it. All I've watched him do for over ten years is *run*." She beamed at Evelyne. "And now he has you. The both of you. Do you mind?" She held her hand over Evelyne's stomach.

Evelyne shook her head, and Bianca put a hand on the swell of baby.

"I would so like to be his anchor. I'm not sure…" Evelyne struggled against the need to lay all her fears out on this woman she barely knew. This woman who would always be just a little bit more dedicated to her actual son than to Evelyne. She forced herself to smile. "He's been very good to me. I hope I'm as good to him."

"Let me tell you, Evelyne. *That* is a good first step to a loving, successful marriage." She said it so approvingly, Evelyne felt buoyed, even knowing the marriage wasn't real and likely would never be.

Even knowing Gabriel didn't love her so there was no *loving* marriage on the horizon.

But she was beginning to realize that she didn't just like him or enjoy him. She *loved* him. The man he was, even when he was trying to hold himself apart. His strength, his desire to protect. His intelligence and irreverence when he wasn't so worried about protection. He was just…exactly what she wanted.

Oh, he would not like her being in love with him. Not at all.

But there was nothing to be done about it now. Except decide how to deal with it. But first, dinner.

Evelyne swallowed at the lump in her throat, blinked away the moisture that threatened to fall. She straightened her shoulders. "Shall we walk down to dinner together?"

"I would like that."

CHAPTER TWELVE

"I LIKE YOUR WIFE."

Gabriel tried to smile instead of tense at his father's warm approval. "She is…" He watched her move around the room, talking to people at this interminable coronation where people wanted to congratulate him on his earldom and he wanted to jump out a window.

But Evelyne positively glowed. She spoke to anyone and everyone. Despite the baby bump, she seemed to simply glide through the room. People responded to her. They lit up right back. She had a warmth about her that Alexandre and Ines could not quite pull off.

Father chuckled, reminding Gabriel he was standing there, then patted him on the back.

"Your mother was worried this was some sort of…ploy to help Alexandre out, but it's clear you quite enjoy her."

Enjoy. Obsess. Was there a difference? "She is having my child."

Father made a noncommittal kind of sound Gabriel did not know what to do with. "Well, with all these changes to Alis thanks to Alexandre's rule, and a child on the way, your mother and I are pleased we will be able to spend more time with you and your new family here."

Family. Gabriel tried not to grimace at the word. At

the idea that he would never be able to create the kind of family his parents had. That nothing would ever be safe if he let himself fall too deep into it all.

Still…

"I am glad you two will be able to make the trip more often. Evelyne is quite excited by the idea of our son having such good grandparents."

"I'm not sure how you spoil a prince rotten when you aren't royalty, but we'll figure it out."

Gabriel smiled in spite of himself. Though he tried not to look forward, to imagine what it would be like to have a son, to watch his parents be grandparents, he could not deny that making his parents happy always eased something inside of him.

But more, the *easing* came from the fact that Evelyne was now making her way toward them. Dangerous, dangerous woman.

"It is a good thing, son," his father said, somewhat cryptically by Gabriel's estimation. "Not always easy. Certainly not something you can skate through, but it is good."

Gabriel looked down at his father. *Skate through* felt a bit like an accusation.

Before he could decide what to say, Evelyne approached them.

"I hope you are enjoying yourself, Mr. Marti. Pardon me, Manuel."

"It is so good to be home, Your Highness, and not worry for my or my family's safety. Your brother will be a good king and make Alis the country I remember as a boy, I have no doubts." He turned to Gabriel and grinned. "And my son shall be quite the earl."

She beamed at him. "I have the utmost faith in the both of them."

"As do I. If you'll excuse me, I must find my wife. Make sure some young man hasn't tried to abscond with her." He gave Evelyne a little bow and then moved off.

Gabriel watched Evelyne watch his father go. She had a bright smile on her face. No signs of exhaustion when no doubt she had to be. She had been running herself hard these past few days. It was clear she was determined to take some pressure off Alexandre's shoulders.

She finally looked up at him, her smile bright and her eyes full of happiness. "I love them," she said emphatically.

Gabriel made a noncommittal noise, realized it sounded like the one his father had made. Would his son take on this tradition?

Would Gabriel know how to handle the weight of that? Ever?

Evelyne took his hand in hers and gave him a bit of a tug forward. "I am afraid you are required by princess law to dance for at least one song with me."

"Are you not tired yet?"

"Not yet. Wired. I'm sure I'll crash when it's all over, but for now I would like to dance with my husband."

Husband. It was a farce, but the more Evelyne acted like it was real, the more it *felt* real. And he had to do a better job of keeping that wall up between them. Some kind of *formality.*

But she led him to the dance floor, and he did not know how to deny her when she looked so happy. He had promised Alexandre that he would *ensure* her happiness.

And he *wanted* to. "You look beautiful. I have not been able to take my eyes off you."

"I know." She moved in easy rhythm, that content and somewhat smug smile never leaving her face as he pulled her close for the dance. "I like having your eyes on me."

That ever-present heat crackled between them. He thought if this did not exist, perhaps it would not all feel so perilous. If he simply *liked* her. But he did not know how to save her from this combination of every feeling—like and lust and need and frustration and this strange, bubbling lightness that reminded him far too much of hope. So much like when he'd been a young man, but worse somehow. Deeper and more complex.

What was there to hope for here? That he somehow controlled himself for the rest of his life and never did anything violent and dangerous in an obsessive rage? Never reminded her of her evil father?

What impossible amount of control would appear out of nowhere considering an impossible lack of one had led him here?

"I think I felt the baby move earlier," she said as they easily moved on the dance floor to the music. "You're going to call me silly, but I swear I felt this flutter of him when Alexandre announced you earl."

"Yes, I will call you silly. If you felt anything, I'm sure it was coincidence."

"Well, I will choose to consider it a son's approval of his father."

"Ridiculous."

She laughed and lay her head against his shoulder on a content sigh. "I knew you would say that."

They danced for the rest of the song and into the next.

For the first time today, amid the chaos and attention and stress, he found himself relaxing. He held her close and enjoyed the bump of their child between them.

He did not allow himself to think of the way she spoke to the baby growing inside her, the way she thought a *fetus* would hear the worlds *earl* and do some little internal jump for joy. He was afraid if he thought too much about any of it, fell beneath that surface he was trying so desperately to hold on to, all he would create was ruin.

He needed space, and with the celebration winding down, and in her condition, he knew he could find it.

"Come, let me take you to bed." He cleared his throat. "To *sleep*."

She tilted her head up to study him. Smiled. "Perhaps I should not like to sleep."

He wanted to smile back. He wanted to get lost in the gold flecks in her eyes. He wanted so many things.

But he kept that wall up, that detachment. He fought with everything he had to keep that erected.

He made their excuses, escorted her back to her rooms and right to the bed—not for anything but *rest*.

"Sit," he ordered her.

She looked up at him through her lashes. "I only follow orders if I like where they're going to lead."

"They're going to lead to rest. You've pushed yourself these past few days. Fine enough if it were just yourself, but you are carrying around an extra human being."

"Boring," she muttered, but she sat down on the bed as he'd ordered.

He knelt and enjoyed the way her breath caught in spite of himself. But he was *not* giving in to the nagging want that hounded him constantly. He was going to ensure she got some rest.

He undid the fanciful buckle of her heels and removed one shoe and set it aside.

"Gabriel?"

He glanced up at her, saw there was a seriousness in her dark gaze that had him pausing. He did not encourage her to continue, but he watched her face as wariness crept into him.

"What happened when you were younger?"

He stiffened in spite of himself. He didn't know what she was getting at, except that of course he knew. He removed the other shoe and got to his feet. "You'll have to be a bit more specific." He picked them both up and walked over to her closet.

"The thing that changed you. That Alexandre saved you from. Your mother mentioned a change. I think they're one and the same, and I think I should know what they are."

He turned to face her slowly. She sat on the bed, a beautiful, stunning delight. He wanted to touch her, glut himself in her, over and over again forever.

He could distract her with that, avoid this question, but it would not be avoided forever, he knew. She simply wouldn't let him avoid it forever, and then what?

Did he lie? Did he get angry? Or did he do the one thing he'd never really done—because Alexandre knew what had happened because he'd been there, witnessed it. Gabriel had never had to explain it.

Perhaps…he should. Perhaps this had been the answer all along. Instead of a secret to hide, a tool to keep her from falling any deeper into accepting this obsession that would only hurt them all.

She would be frightened by this story, and he did not want that. With a bone-deep reaction, he did not want her to look at him differently than she did now.

But wants were dangerous, weren't they? If she didn't hero worship him, perhaps they could solve this problem. He wouldn't run away, she was right. He would not desert her or their son, but if there could be barriers...

To keep them both safe. They could have a marriage like Alexandre and Ines. For the greater good. A workable partnership, but none of this passion, none of these time bombs ticking inside him.

He had been depending on himself and himself alone to have control, but if Evelyne knew, if she understood, perhaps their control *together* would solve this.

He held on to this hope with a surge of determination. It *had* to be the answer. So he went about telling her something he'd never truly explained to anyone.

"I met a girl during my last year at St. Olga. She was a little bit older than I was. Perhaps a little bit more... worldly to my more privileged life. But I was quite taken with her."

"What was her name?" Evelyne asked softly.

"Gia."

"I hate her." She did *not* say this softly, and there was something...amusing about the simple jealousy that shouldn't exist and certainly shouldn't be *funny*. Nothing about this was a laughing manner.

He scrubbed his hands over his face, trying to put himself back there so he could adequately convey the depths and breadth of his lack of control, lack of sanity and decision-making.

This *thing* inside him that endangered her. *And* their son.

"She was beautiful, charming, fun. She...was exciting. Everything about her. I wanted to spend...all my time with her and the worlds she opened up, but she worked at the café we studied at, so she had responsibilities of her own. So there was...pining, I suppose."

Evelyne only scowled. In any other situation, Evelyne's expression would have amused him. She looked a bit like a spoiled princess, thwarted, when she was none of those things.

"But when she did have time for me, we enjoyed each other. Early on in our relationship, she confided in me that she had a stalker. A man from her neighborhood who followed her around, harassed her, though he'd never touched her. I promised to protect her. Happy to do anything for her, feel powerful and..." A savior. Just as he'd felt with Evelyne.

There was simply no way he could fool himself into thinking he could handle all that warred inside him when he dove beneath the surface of feeling. He would hold on too tight. He would scare and hurt her.

He had perhaps saved Gia from one awful thing, but he had only introduced another. How could he expect any different when it came to Evelyne?

He would be the monster Gia had once told him he was. Because he *was* that, deep down. His need to protect or save was only a function of some dark, horrible part of his psyche.

"As much as I don't relish thinking of you protecting

any woman you slept with aside from me, that's hardly something to be ashamed of. You wanted to help. You always want to help. You're a good man, Gabriel."

He shook his head. "You are very, *very* far off, Evelyne. I... There is the same violence in me that was in your father."

"Don't be ridiculous, Gabriel. My God."

"It is true. I do not revel in it the way he did. I am not *proud* of it as he was, but it is there. One day I came to pick Gia up from her shift, and he was there. Her stalker had cornered her, put his hands on her, was trying to get her into his car."

Gabriel hated to relive this, but surely she had to see what a risk she ran. If he could get it through to her that surface was all he could ever be, then both her and their child would be safe from this dangerous, destructive thing inside him.

"I do not remember everything in that moment. Just the rage. In the aftermath, I know I pulled him off her, and I..." Gabriel swallowed. "I cannot say I fought him, because he didn't fight back. I simply beat him."

"But he was hurting her," Evelyne said softly.

Gabriel shook his head. "Yes, but there were alternatives. Beating this man did not save her. She stood there, watching. Violence on top of violence. She was screaming at me to stop by the end. Thank God for Alexandre. He waded in, pulled me off, and asked if I wished to be the same kind of man as your father. It was the only thing that saved me from killing that man."

Evelyne was quiet for a very long time. He did not dare look at her. This story would have to change things for her. It had changed things for *him. Everything.*

"Gia called me a monster. And I *was* a monster. Even Alex saw it. He just knew how to stop it."

Still Evelyne said nothing. Gabriel realized he was breathing heavily, winded almost. Like something was happening inside him. Some great force of change.

He shook his head, pushed the heel of his palm to his chest. There was no change. Only the truth. "It is all I have in me, Evelyne. Obsession or nothing. Drowning or skating. There is no middle ground for me. And once the switch is flipped, I cannot be trusted to make the correct decisions."

She slid off the bed, moved over to him even as he held up a hand to ward her off. She took that hand in her tiny one.

"Gabriel, how silly to think so."

He pulled away from her hand, took steps back. Regarded her with as much ice as he had left in him. "I was hoping you'd be mature enough to understand."

She regarded him with that royal superiority he found infuriating. Because it made her seem infinitely *mature*. "You were hoping I'd run away. Since, this time around, you cannot."

"You'd be surprised what I could do, Evelyne."

She shook her head. "Perhaps this feeling you have inside you is true. I cannot believe it. I cannot buy into this story you've told yourself. Or perhaps Gia and Alexandre told you. You are no monster. You are *nothing* like my father. Rushing into *save* is not wrong."

"It is if you are willing to do worse." Would he have had any remorse in killing that man? In the moment, there had been *none*. Not until Alex had told him what he was in danger of becoming.

All because he had wanted to save Gia and make her love him.

Evelyne sighed heavily. "I cannot see this the way you do, Gabriel. I have been the woman in that scenario. And while Alexandre stepped in and stopped it when he could, I would have not called you a monster if you'd done to my father what you did to that man. I would have cheered. And I cannot find a way to feel guilty about that."

He shook his head. "You don't..." Of course, he couldn't say she didn't understand. Even though she *didn't*. She could only see this from her own eyes. Not from his. Not from Gia's. Not from Alexandre's. So while she might understand what it felt like to have someone step in and save her, she did not understand it to his degree.

"Perhaps you thought this story would change my mind about you, but it doesn't. And more, it doesn't change our reality. You have a responsibility to all the people you love, and no matter how you might wish to, you cannot walk away from it."

People you love... He looked at her in horror as that clutching feeling in his chest threatened to make it fully impossible to breathe. "Do you think I love you?"

"No," she said, with a sadness that cut through him like a knife. "But I think if you let yourself fall from the surface, you could. I have certainly fallen in love with you."

The pain of that simple, easy revelation was unbearable. She couldn't... "Evelyne, what a mistake."

She shrugged. "People make mistakes. I have seen the width and breadth of mistakes people can make. For good reasons and for bad. I cannot... I cannot feel the way you feel about this. I'm sorry. I know you want me to, but I remember what it feels like to be eighteen and wanting to exact revenge. Older, in fact. If you recall, not that long ago, I was ready for poor Jordi to suffer my father's consequences because he had refused to run away with me."

"That is not the same."

"You're right. It's worse. Jordi simply disappointed me. He didn't try to *harm* me." She lifted an eyebrow. "Do you recall what my father was capable of?"

He shook his head. Yes, the king had been dangerous, and yes, Evelyne's flippant remark about blaming Jordi for her disappearance had not been a decision made with clearheaded thinking, but she hadn't *insisted*. She hadn't actually planned or plotted or done anything about it.

"Do you think I fear you? Because when you were young you hurt someone in an effort to save a woman you loved?" Evelyne demanded. "You think I fear *you* as much or more than I feared the man who *actually* put his hands on me in violence? His own daughter? Not a stranger harming others?"

Gabriel could not look at her. He hated when she brought her abuse up as if it was such a simple fact of life. But she was changing the subject, and he could not let her. "You should fear me. That potential that marred your childhood is inside me. I saw it. I felt it. You must fear me, Evelyne. It is our only hope."

She shrugged, so nonchalant. "I will not."

"And if the monster I have learned to repress threatens our son because that chain breaks? Perhaps I would never lay a hand on you or him, but that is not the only way to traumatize someone with violence. Gia saw a monster in me. She could never look at me again. She was right."

She heaved out a sigh. Frustration dug into her expression but not what needed to—that fear, concern, worry. *Anything*.

"I lived with a monster all my life, Gabriel," she said very directly. "Monsters do not have remorse. They do not concern themselves with the feelings of others. They do not listen to friends who intervene. You can try to convince me that somehow you are a threat, but I *know* threats."

"You cannot know every threat simply because your father beat you, Evelyne."

She inhaled deeply, eventually nodded. Some agreement that allowed a ray of hope to pierce through all this worry. "You are right."

Thank *God*, he thought, sure the heavy weight on his shoulders was just relief.

"But let me ask you this, Gabriel. Do you think I would have done anything but applaud if you'd been the one to kill my father, even in front of me?"

Gabriel didn't know how to fully engage with that question. It was different. She was conflating things, but he did not know how to get that through her thick skull. Because clearly it was just stubbornness that she didn't understand.

She couldn't possibly be *right* about things he'd been living with for over ten years. She could not see more clearly. She didn't understand.

"You wanted to protect a woman you loved. I cannot fault you for that. I cannot fault you for being angry enough to do something about it."

"I would have killed—"

"You do not know what you would have done, because you did not get the chance. Alexandre may have stopped you with his words, but *you* allowed those words to matter, Gabriel."

"I allowed nothing. I still *wanted* it, Evelyne. But I knew it would be the end of my life, and I did not want to hurt my parents. Thanks to Alexandre, I finally put something else ahead of my impulses, but only because of his interference."

"I suppose it's quite *simple* then," she said, the word *simple* dripping with sarcasm. "If you are in the wrong, then so am I. Because that doesn't bother me. Do you know how many plans I had to kill my own father? How I would have done it if I'd thought I could actually accomplish it?"

He wanted to shout. She was so frustrating. And purposefully so. Her wanting to kill her abuser was not the same. Could not be the same. "You…do not understand. You are young and naïve. This is more complex."

Evelyne had the nerve to roll her eyes. "Ah, yes, back to my simplistic views on life. How's this for simple? I think *you* are naïve, Gabriel. I think you stopped maturing in that moment. All your surface, all your…keep yourself apart. All it is is a childish desire to control… how you feel. How *I* feel. Instead of deal."

He found himself speechless. She was *wrong*. He didn't have to engage with her accusation to know she was just… flat-out dead wrong. Confused. *Sheltered* for all the pain she'd dealt with.

She would not accept this. She was too stubborn. Too certain of herself. Too used to having her own opinions verified. She could not understand.

It was unfathomable.

"Good night, Evelyne. Get some sleep."

She laughed, the sound a bit caustic. Harsh enough he felt himself wince. "Good night, Gabriel."

And he could have sworn he heard her say, as he left her room, *run away again*.

But surely he was imagining things.

CHAPTER THIRTEEN

EVELYNE HAD *NOT* slept well. She had been worked up in too many different ways. First and foremost, angry at the rigid thinking that didn't allow Gabriel to *understand*. That he would find fault with *her* rather than question his own misguided feeling.

But there was a sadness, a regret, underneath all that. Because she didn't know how to get through to him. She had known his issues had kept this barrier between them, but she hadn't understood how deep and how long he'd held these issues. Nursed them.

She wanted to have hope that when their baby was born, he would see life for what it was: complicated and difficult. There was always guilt and wrong choices, but on the other hand, there was always hope and good choices too. That he was not forever cursed by something he hadn't even done.

She did not understand punishing oneself for a choice they *hadn't* made.

But now she worried even the birth of their child would not soften him if her confession of love hadn't so much as slowed him in his tracks. If he could not admit he loved her, or accept she loved him, he would always hold this wall between them. Out of fear—not for himself, of course, but for those he loved.

And he did love, whether he admitted it or not. Just as she loved.

Funnily enough, this was her concern. That the deep abiding love he felt would be their undoing. It would maintain that wall, even in the face of their child. Perhaps especially in the face of their child.

Because he thought himself a monster.

He wasn't. At *all*, but he'd made her afraid now, that if they went on as they were, their child would only get glimpses of the real Gabriel. Forever. The loving man who existed underneath his need to be distanced from such feelings would be all they ever knew.

She tried to look at it from an unbiased point of view. Maybe she was letting her feelings for Gabriel soften the blow of this admission of his. Maybe he really would have killed that man had Alexandre not intervened. Maybe he *was* a monster, and because that was what she'd grown up with, she loved a monster. Maybe these were her own traumas and issues at play.

But Evelyne just kept coming back to what she'd grown up with. Men who wielded power and force to get what they wanted. Familiar? Yes, but not what she sought out.

This was not in Gabriel's heart, no matter how much he feared it. She had been the driving force in everything between them. Not *him*. And everything he'd done for her had either been in service to Alexandre, her, or his need to keep that wall between them erected.

Even when he'd been mean to her, tried to discard her, he hadn't done it with his fists. He hadn't even really done any damage with his words.

Or does love and lust cloud your judgment?

She didn't have any answers, but the idea of clouding her judgment gave her an idea. There was someone's judgment she always trusted. She got dressed for the day, forced herself to eat despite not feeling hungry at all.

"I will take care of you no matter what," she murmured to the baby.

Then she headed for Alexandre's office. Despite his assistant's many protestations that the king had an important meeting soon that he was readying for, Evelyne walked right in, closed the door behind her before his assistant could follow and interfere.

She flipped the lock.

"Alex. I need you to tell me about what happened with this Gia woman."

Alex looked up from his computer. He blinked once or twice, no doubt to focus on her instead of the screen. "Pardon me?"

"This Gia woman Gabriel was involved with when you both were young. This man he beat so badly. I want to hear your version."

Alexandre was quiet for some time. When he finally spoke, it was with an annoying lack of emotion. "It is not my place to tell his story."

Evelyne shook her head. "*He* told me his story. And expects me to...fear him now, or something. I want your point of view. I want your side of the story as an observer. So I can understand. So I can...figure this out."

Alexandre studied her for quite some time. When he asked his question, it was completely devoid of emotion. "Do you fear Gabriel?"

She rolled her eyes. "Don't be ridiculous. He is almost as good and honest as you."

"You say that like an insult, Evelyne."

She merely raised a brow.

Alexandre sighed, pinched the bridge of his nose. Eventually he got to his feet, came around the desk and took her arm. He moved her around his desk, nudged her to take the seat he'd left.

"You've been on your feet all week. You should be taking today to rest." It wasn't just admonishment. It was meant to be a kind of distraction.

It would not work. "Alexandre, tell me what happened back then. I know he says you stopped him from murder."

Alexandre shook his head. "I do not know that it would have been murder. It's...complicated. And in the past."

"Not his past. He's so convinced he's a danger. Something that's patently ridiculous as the worst he's ever done is speak a few harsh words to me—out of this same fear that he is bad. I just don't see it. He is so good, and I *love* him, Alexandre. I truly do."

She thought of the way he'd reacted to those words. By not really reacting. By essentially despairing of her. Calling it a *mistake*. But he did not seem blindsided by the admission. He did not deny those feelings.

"I've had my reservations about the two of you, but I am glad to hear you say so. You both deserve...the warmth in each other."

For a moment, she considered asking about Ines, about *warmth*—or lack thereof, but she could only deal with one problematic relationship at a time.

"So what am I missing?" Evelyne demanded. Maybe

begged. "What isn't he telling me? Why can't I under-stand this?"

"What was his version of events?" Alex asked, very patiently.

She went through what Gabriel had told her, hoping she didn't leave anything out. She used the same words he'd used. Described it just as Gabriel had, without any of her own commentary.

"Do you feel like you are the only thing that saved him?" she asked.

Per usual, Alexandre took his time answering, but this was how Evelyne knew he would tell her the truth, not just pat her head and tell her not to worry.

"It is impossible to say. He did harm that man, but con-sidering the man had been dragging Gia into his *car*, I do not see what the alternative in the moment would have been. I always thought… He was much too hard on him-self. In that moment, there was only reaction."

"You told him he was the same as Father."

Alexandre's eyebrows drew together. "That is *not* what I said. I told him the man was unconscious—something he didn't realize because he was trying to neutralize a threat. All I said was that continuing was something our father would do."

It was Evelyne's turn to frown. It was essentially what Gabriel had said Alex had said, but…the way Alex said it now was…softer. Not an accusation. A reminder.

"Gia called him a monster."

Alexandre's expression flattened. A hint of his rarely freed temper flickered in his eyes for a moment. "He did not tell me that."

"And that is what he has thought of himself all these

years. You were there, but you do not believe him a monster, or he would not have been in our lives. You certainly wouldn't have trusted him to save me from marrying the general."

"We know what a monster looks like, Evelyne."

"That's what I told him." Feeling despair that this wasn't actually getting her anywhere, just the same conclusions, she looked up at Alex imploringly. "Why won't he listen to me?"

Alexandre moved across the room, and back, pacing with his hands clasped behind his back. As though he was going over it all in his mind. "It has been many years, Evelyne. I have not been able to get through to him. I assumed marriage meant... He had dealt with it finally."

Evelyne looked down at her baby bump in spite of herself. She could tell Alexandre the truth of how her and Gabriel had come to be married, but it seemed neither here nor there. "I suppose a child...brought those feelings back instead."

Alexandre made a noise Evelyne didn't know how to characterize, and worried if she asked, he might start poking into places she didn't want him to be. Like how exactly she had come to marry his best friend.

"Regardless, Gabriel is not a monster," Evelyne said firmly. "He was not in the wrong."

"I do not agree with his characterization of events, but there *is* violence in him, Evelyne. I have seen it. I cannot deny that."

"To protect. Not like Father. *I* would have killed Father if given the chance. What does that make me?"

"Human, Evelyne," he said very gently.

"You wouldn't have."

Alex sighed. "It was certainly a thought that occurred to me a time or two. I am not immune. But I always knew…it would create more problems than it would ever solve. And lo and behold, a blood clot did the work for me instead."

"God bless it."

Alexandre's mouth almost curved.

Evelyne pushed to her feet, grabbed her brother's hands, squeezed. "How do I get through to him, Alex?"

He met her gaze with a sadness that had her heart sinking. "If I knew, I would have done it by now."

Evelyne wouldn't allow herself to cry, but she certainly *felt* like crying. Why should this be hopeless? Why should a good man be so convinced he was not one? When she'd grown up with men convinced of their righteousness that was nothing but madness and cruelty.

The door opened and Alexandre's assistant poked his head in. His expression was pinched, his gaze accusingly on Evelyne. "Your Majesty. The diplomats are *waiting*."

"Yes, I will be right there," Alex muttered, waving him away. "I'm sorry. I do have to go. And I'm sorry I could not give you a better answer, Evelyne. Perhaps time and this child will be what he needs. I have never given up on him. I know you won't either."

Give up on him. She couldn't imagine what would have to happen for that to occur.

Alexandre leaned in, gave her a rare show of affection with a brush of lips against her hair. "You will make an excellent mother, Ev. Your care for people is truly a gift. I hope Gabriel can accept it." He pulled back. "If you'll excuse me." Alexandre strode from the room, leaving Evelyne standing there moved. Teary.

And considering.

Alexandre had never given up on Gabriel. She knew just talking to his parents that they had never done so either, even if they didn't know about what had happened. No one who really loved him had ever really given *up* on him.

So if no one had, then maybe that was the answer, the things that would change his mind. Not the answer she *wanted*. Nothing warm, kind, supportive like she wanted to be.

Maybe this time someone needed to be strong enough to choose an answer that would hurt.

"But it might be the only thing to do," she said, running her hands over her baby bump.

She was going to have to give Gabriel exactly what he wanted.

And hope he realized how wrong it was.

CHAPTER FOURTEEN

GABRIEL SPENT THE next few days sleeping in the sitting room and considering his options. He was surprised and, if he was honest with himself, a bit disappointed that Evelyne had let him be.

She did not come to him to make arguments and further propose he wasn't a monster. She did not try to entice him back into her bed.

If he saw her, it was only in glimpses. They didn't eat together, sleep together, or even attend royal meetings together.

He thought she spent most of her time with Ines, but he wasn't certain. It ate at him, but he told himself it was for the best. Perhaps he had gotten through to her.

And wouldn't that be a boon?

He told himself it was indeed, even as he looked for her around every corner, at every table, and even in the sitting room at night. Because no matter how he tried to convince himself he had *won*, everything was unsettled.

It was a bit like watching a storm approach in that house in Maine. You could see it in the distance, feel it crackle with power, long before it ever made it to shore. In the peace between now and then, you could almost convince yourself this was it. This was the new normal.

When he came back to the sitting room one evening to find her sitting on the sofa, reading a book, he knew the storm had reached shore. Because she was never here, certainly this late, when she knew he might arrive to take his proper place on the couch.

But she didn't look like a storm. She was dressed in a flowy ensemble the color of bubblegum. It somehow made everything gold in her shimmer brightly, including her hair piled atop her head in some large clip.

She held up a finger to him, continued to read her book, then once she'd finished the page, presumably, folded the edge of the page over, closed the book and set it down on her lap. She met his gaze with hands folded over the book.

She looked so regal sitting there regarding him with a cool kind of detachment. Radiant and beautiful and like she alone ran the world.

He wanted to kneel at her feet, a great howling impulse he ruthlessly fought back.

His wants would serve neither of them. *Obviously.*

She did not invite him to sit, and he felt much like he had in Alexandre's office those weeks ago, explaining himself while Alex sat behind his desk. She had certainly picked up a few tricks from her brother.

"I have given your story much thought," she said by way of greeting.

Ah, so she was here to convince him he was wrong. Satisfaction wound through him. Not because she was finally fighting it, of course, but because… Because… Well, the fact it had taken her days to come up with a suitable rebuttal just proved his point, didn't it?

He would be damn glad to be proven right, he was certain of it. And how could she argue with it? She couldn't.

"Perhaps you are right."

He opened his mouth to argue with her before he realized she'd...said he was right.

She wasn't fighting. She wasn't telling him he was good. That his violent tendencies weren't unimportant.

She was saying he was *right*.

He did not have the words to respond to *that*.

"As much as I am not convinced, how can I be more certain of your feelings, the truth of you, than you are?" she said, with the wave of a hand. "You live in your body, your mind. I do not. Perhaps there is no evidence for *me* to believe this monster exists inside of you, but if you have determined it does, I cannot argue with you." She held his gaze, still cool and direct without a hint of any other emotion. "I have to accept it."

Accept... He was having trouble keeping up with her. She spoke so...decisively, dispassionately, as though they were having a meeting about royal protocol. Not...dissolving whatever this was that existed between them.

"We cannot have the marriage annulled, not with a child on the way. Not with how it might reflect on Alexandre and our son's future reign," she said flatly. "So I'm afraid that is out of the question."

"Annulled." The word echoed through him like some sort of bullet—causing damage as it ricocheted through his insides. Who had said anything about...

"And having grown up without a mother, I do not think I want my son to grow up without a father. Though Alexandre would be a fine stand-in. I do not think you wish to banish yourself from your child's life completely."

"Stand-in." She was talking about him...not being involved in their child's life? Talking about all this ending? *Banish yourself?* No... That was not exactly what he'd meant. Exactly.

It is for the best, some vicious voice inside him whispered. But that whisper had nothing on the howl of pain that echoed through his soul. Here she was, their child tucked up inside her, talking about annulments and banishments as though they were...choices on a menu. Considered. Rejected. Of no real import.

"But we do need to come up with *something*, don't we? To handle this...problem as you see it. I think I have come up with an answer. If you watch Ines and Alexandre, everyone thinks they are married, and they are legally, but they don't...behave as a couple. They sleep in separate rooms. They busy themselves with different parts of being king and queen. They are cordial, they support one another, but there is no...love. And certainly no passion. I have decided we will follow in their example."

She had *decided*. The princess's decree. And she left no room for argument, for this crumbling inside him. She simply kept talking about *plans*.

"We will move chambers. There are adjoining rooms we will settle into. We will keep our lives separate in private and come together when needed in public. When the baby comes, he will be with us until and unless we feel the need for a nanny. You may go back to traveling, using work as an excuse. You can spend time in Italy if you see fit. You do not need to clear it with me, because we will live separately. Your responsibility will only be to your son, your friend and your title. Not me."

They already had been living separately, so this was

hardly a blow, even if he could not get that message through to his body. It throbbed with a pain he could not seem to talk himself out of.

"You must be available for royal events. You must still behave as a married earl. I hope it won't be too much of a hardship for you, but it is too late to undo that which is already done. Not without hurting Alexandre or the kingdom. At least for now. But within those constraints, you may…do whatever you need to do to keep this *monster* to yourself."

She did not say it with derision. She was being perfectly reasonable. So reasonable she didn't even seem like herself. So reasonable… She was right. This was all well and good, and the best course of action.

Still, he stood, without the words to agree, to accept, feeling a bit like a soldier stuck in no-man's-land.

"Do you have anything to say?" she asked. Dry-eyed and detached. She was not being mean or cruel or kind or anything. She was… She was treating this like a business. Which he should appreciate and do in kind, but when he spoke his voice was little more than a rasp.

"And when the baby comes?"

For the first time, she did not meet his gaze. She looked down at her belly, picked something off the fabric of her shirt. "We will have to reconvene and discuss next steps once we understand the reality of having a newborn. If you feel yourself some kind of danger to our child…"

She let that hang there, the sentence not fully spoken, but the meaning clear. Her mouth curved, but it was not a smile. Not from Evelyne. She raised her gaze back to his. "This is what you wish, is it not?"

He stared at her, those dark eyes, never looking away

from him. She had taken days to think this through, and she had decided to agree with him, just as he'd hoped. Just as he'd *known* was right.

But he hadn't expected it, so he did not know how to feel. And he realized… He did not know what he wished, except to protect her. And this would accomplish that. These dangerous, uncontrollable feelings inside him could not win, could not *hurt* if they essentially lived separate lives. If *she* agreed to these separate lives.

She hadn't just agreed. She'd planned it all out. Nothing could be better. Even if his body somehow felt as though it had been cracked in half, opened in front of her, everything inside him spilling out at her feet.

But he let *nothing* out. He had to control all that whirled inside him. "Yes, this is ideal."

She gave a sharp nod. "I will always be grateful you brought me our son. The future king of Alis." She moved to get to her feet, but here she was not quite so graceful or elegant. She struggled to push herself up, and before he'd thought it through, he moved to help her.

One hand on her elbow offering leverage, one hand somehow landing on her stomach. For a moment, they both froze in the warmth of physical connection. And then something under his hand seemed to…jerk.

He pulled his hand back in reflex, then immediately pressed it back to the same spot on her stomach. "Was that…"

"He kicked." She let out a little laugh, looked up at him now with the vibrant shine of *life* in her eyes. "I have been feeling flutters but nothing so certain as that yet, though all the books say I should start. And now…"

He could not help but grin down at her. A kick. It

was so…real. So bafflingly real. A reminder that in short months this life inside her would be *outside*. Real and his. He would hold his son in his arms and…

Or he would be miles away. In Italy. Living a separate life.

He watched her swallow, look away. Because it did not matter how beautiful the idea of holding their son in his arms was. Their lives would be separate. Everything would be separate.

For Evelyne and the boy's own good. And since it was, he should start now.

He took two careful steps back, clasped his hands behind him. He regarded her with the same cool detachment she had been giving him. Or tried. "I think I shall fly to Italy tonight. Handle some business."

She did not say anything at first. Just stood very still. Eventually she inclined her head though. "Of course. Have a safe journey, Gabriel." She even smiled at him.

He could not seem to manage the same. "Stay well, Your Highness."

And he left. The palace and Alis and *her*.

For her own good.

Definitely not for his.

Evelyne cried herself to sleep. That night. And the next. And the next. She tried to tell herself all would be well. She had her brother, her sister-in-law and in two months or so she would have her child. She lived in a kingdom no longer ruled by her father.

All was *well*.

She tried to plan. Decorate the nursery. Decide on a name. Focus on the positive parts of the future.

But everything felt as though Gabriel should have some say, even though he had given up his say and gone to *Italy*.

She would have spent all her time alone, wallowing, but Ines insisted on sharing meals, and since she did not often eat with Alexandre, Evelyne felt honor bound to be company for her.

But now both Ines *and* Alexandre joined her in one of the parlors in the evenings. She must not be hiding her misery very well.

"I can require him to return, you know," Alex muttered one evening as he read something on his tablet.

Evelyne looked up at Alexandre. Not only was he watching her, but so was Ines. They were both worried about her. She knew this because they were spending their evenings together. With her, to be sure, but usually they did not simply sit in the parlor like this together.

So she smiled. "I think I should only like you to require his return if it were to throw him in the dungeons."

"I'm sure that can also be arranged," Ines offered, earning her a sharp look from her husband. Which Ines ignored, going back to the blanket she was knitting for the baby.

Evelyne put her hand over her stomach. She felt some movement and tried to be comforted by his existence. Comforted by the reality of *life*.

She was used to not getting what she wanted, wasn't she? A few weeks of having what she wanted shouldn't change things.

"I do not want him forced into anything. He has made his choices. I will make mine." Even if she was struggling to make *any* choice. It didn't matter. She didn't want to think about this. She stood. "I think I shall go to bed," she announced.

And knew their gazes followed her all the way out.

Almost like they knew she was going to cry herself to sleep again.

King Alexandre Enzo Rodrigo Lidia was used to being told what to do. His father had ruled him with an iron fist, and Alexandre had learned how to develop his own sense of duty under the chains of that evil man thanks to his mother. So he liked to think he knew what to do with orders—how to determine if they were the appropriate course of action, if he should give the person doing the ordering the satisfaction of thinking they ordered a prince—now king—or if he would make it clear they had no say over him.

But he did not know what to do with his wife, standing here in this parlor, telling him what to do after Evelyne had trudged away.

"You must interfere," Ines told him, with quite a bit of fire and determination he had never *once* seen from her in these near ten months of marriage.

She never told him anything. Never insisted upon anything. She was usually exactly as he'd expected she'd be, what King Enzo had wanted the princess to be. Beige. Malleable. Deferential. She was such a tiny little thing, Alexandre hadn't given thought to the fact there might be any room for much else.

And now she stood, looking down at him in his chair. Telling him—a *king*—what to do.

He rather wanted to refuse her out of principle, but she was talking about Evelyne and... Well, it was all too clear his sister was miserable, and though he'd seen little of Gabriel, there was no doubt he was the same.

If he knew how to fix it, he supposed he would. The problem was the not knowing. He wasn't about to admit that to his wife.

"And how do you propose I do that? Evelyne has made it clear she does not wish to *make* him do anything."

Ines huffed impatiently. He'd had no idea she could *be* impatient.

"You need to convince him he is not this danger he seems to think. It's utterly ludicrous."

Alex frowned. "Evelyne told you…"

"Evelyne has told me *everything*. Because she is lonely and miserable and heartbroken. She needs a friend, and I have been that for her. And as perhaps the only impartial bystander here, I can tell you with certainty your friend is being an idiot. You must interfere, Alex. For your sister's sake."

She never called him Alex. He did not quite know what to do with this strange turn of events. And he always knew what to do, no matter the turn of events.

Ines inhaled deeply. When she spoke again, she sounded more herself. Her expression was calm, her words rational. "The truth of the matter is, we know what a loveless marriage looks like. We are quite happy to spend our time apart. Evelyne is miserable with Gabriel away. I would wager a guess Gabriel is miserable *being* away. But they cannot quite see past their own misery. *We* can. We can help them. We must."

She did not say *if we cannot be happy, at least they can be*, but he felt it all the same.

"If I require him to come back here, Evelyne does not

need to know it was at my insistence. Perhaps simply spending time together will…"

Ines was shaking her head. "You need to find some way to prove to Gabriel who he really is, not who he thinks he is. He is *your* best friend. You should know how to do this."

Alexandre would not admit he didn't have a clue. And he didn't have to, because Ines whirled away, leaving him alone in the parlor. Chewing over her parting shot. And perhaps this new side of herself she'd shown him.

It wouldn't do to consider that, though. Not when they no longer needed to create an heir. Thanks to Evelyne. And Gabriel.

So he focused on them.

It took him a little bit, but when he saw he had a meeting scheduled in the morning with the general, Alexandre began to form a plan.

CHAPTER FIFTEEN

THE MISSIVE FROM Alexandre was a surprise. Gabriel looked at the email requiring his return for a few days of "royal protocol" meetings and frowned.

Gabriel did not wish to return to Alis. The longer he was away, the more he worried his return would end in… poor choices on his part.

He missed Evelyne like a limb. He wasn't sleeping. His work suffered. His personal assistant had asked—repeatedly—if he should set up a doctor appointment for Gabriel.

No doctor could cure this *sickness* inside him. Nothing could. But if he went back to the palace, what might he convince himself would?

Luckily, though it felt nothing like luck, his reaction to being away only brought home one clear and important point. This pain and suffering proved everything he'd told her. Because if he had a reasonable, rational connection to Evelyne, if love could be normal and safe for him, wouldn't he be handling a separation much better? Perhaps with *some* pain but not feeling as though his very life had ended.

But he was dangerously obsessed, and he had to accept this pain and stay away. For *her* sake.

Except Alexandre was *requiring* his presence now.

What choice did Gabriel have? A king's edict meant he had to obey, particularly now that he was an earl. If he found himself...energized by the flight to France, and perhaps *enjoying* the drive across the border...

He would handle it. By avoiding Evelyne at all costs. Yes, that's what he'd do. No anticipation at seeing her because he *would not*. Perhaps he could even convince Alexandre that whatever needed his attention could be handled in one day and he would not need to spend the night.

He pulled up to the private entrance to the castle, frowned at the three guards who stood there, hands on their weapons, like they were barring entrance.

He got out of his car, handed his keys to the waiting valet. "Is everything all right here?"

The valet looked from the keys to the guards, then bowed and got in the car. Saying nothing. He drove away, leaving Gabriel with the guards.

Concerned that something bad had happened inside the palace, something dangerous or threatening, Gabriel approached the guards quickly. "Gentlemen," he greeted. "Is there a problem?"

They did not answer, but the door behind them opening was an answer. Because out stepped General Vinyes. Dressed in his military regalia. He had been openly critical of Alexandre these past few weeks, but he had not mounted any actual attacks, nor did he defy any of the new king's orders.

The general knew a good thing when he had it, or so Gabriel thought. Gabriel could not imagine what *this* was about though. Nothing good.

"Good afternoon, General. You seem to be in my way."

Gabriel smiled at him. The sharpness in the smile was not likely to be construed as friendly.

"Alas, I am afraid you will have to come with me, Mr. Marti."

"Ah, but it isn't *mister* anymore, is it? I believe you are to address me as *my lord*?" Gabriel hadn't had cause to use his new title, but if ever there was a time to flaunt it, no doubt it would be to this vicious general.

The general's expression darkened. "It has come to my attention that you were the person who kidnapped the princess."

Gabriel studied the man before him. Pompous and smarmy, those were the two main descriptors that came to mind. Him even mentioning Evelyne soured Gabriel's mood even further. "You mean my *wife*?"

"She was not your wife when you illegally absconded with a member of the royal family. We have evidence. You will be arrested."

Gabriel found it odd he wanted to laugh. Instead, he stood where he was and acted bored. Because he was. "Have you brought this evidence to the king? Have you come up with charges?"

"We shall arrest you first." The general's chin moved up. "Once we have, we will present the facts to your *friend*. Even kings have to admit when their friends are in the wrong when presented with evidence. Because if he does not use said evidence to punish you, the people will know."

Gabriel pretended to mull this over. "A word of advice, General? I would not recommend this course of action. Whatever it is you think you're going to accomplish, I can assure you, you won't." The public loved Evelyne. They did *not* love the general. While this plan might cause a bit of a headache for Alexandre, and Gabriel regretted that, he also knew Alex could hardly arrest him for what he'd done at Alex's behest.

Especially when Gabriel was currently *married* to the princess. Perhaps he *was* going to have to see her after all. It was certainly dread he felt at that realization.

Not hope.

The general leaned in, his eyes flinty and soulless. "If the king were still alive, you'd be tried for treason. And sentenced to death."

"What a shame he's six feet under instead," Gabriel returned. He took a step to move around the guards, but their grips on the guns changed. Moved.

Aimed.

"I do not think the princess should be married to such a man. Perhaps there's even a bit of Stockholm Syndrome happening. The king will sort it out, but you must be held while we do so."

Gabriel looked from the guns, to the general.

"Have no concerns, *my lord*. I will ensure your...wife's safety in the ensuing weeks as we sort this out."

It was the most veiled of threats, but it was a threat. Gabriel looked down at the man, wondering what on earth gave him the gall to punch so completely out of his weight class.

"Mark my words, *General*, if you so much as look at my wife the wrong way, I will end you."

"Your friendship with the prince—"

"The king, General. You forget yourself. And I am an earl now, as I have reminded you." He smiled at the older man, though the expression held nothing but malice. "I believe that ranks me above you these days. Now get out of my way before this becomes an embarrassment."

"You do not give me orders." The general stood a little taller, the men held their guns a little tighter.

Gabriel surveyed the soldiers. The gleam in the general's eye. And in a flash, saw this for what it was.

Bait. A trap. If he reacted as he wanted to—that roiling physical violence inside him—he *would* be arrested, perhaps even attacked if the general's expression was anything to go by. And while Alexandre could easily absolve him of kidnapping charges, clearing him of attacking a general might require some more work.

Gabriel did not wish to require this of his friend. It would be a mess, and it would risk things for Alex that need not be risked.

No matter how Gabriel would like to plow his fist into the general's nose.

Instead, he smiled once more. He breathed. And he spoke, very carefully. "I suggest you let me go talk to our king without such theatrics." And with that, Gabriel walked past them. There was no point in giving them the satisfaction of a fight. Though his fists clenched in spite of himself.

They did not stop him, and they did not follow. Gabriel could *feel* the general's angry gaze on him, but nothing happened. It had been posturing at best, though Alexandre would need to know about it.

And nip it in the bud.

Gabriel marched his way through the palace and though he ached to see Evelyne, he would not give in to that. He was here at Alexandre's behest, and he had to warn his friend about a general with a vendetta.

He was *not* here to see his wife.

So he went straight for Alex's office, though his gaze moved toward the hallway that would take him to his— to *Evelyne's* rooms. Or maybe she'd moved by now, to their connecting rooms. For their separate private lives.

Alexandre's assistant greeted him as he approached. He gestured toward the office door. "The king will see you now."

"Thank you," Gabriel murmured, letting himself in. He shut the door behind him, lest the general decided he wanted to attend the meeting.

Alex flicked a glance up from his computer. "Thank you for coming so quickly, Gabriel," he greeted. He typed a few more words before shutting his laptop. He stood. "There are some things that needed to be done in person."

Gabriel nodded. "Very well, but first we must discuss the general."

"Vinyes? What of him?" Alex looked down at some papers on his desk, eased a hip against it.

"He claims he has evidence that I kidnapped the princess. He made some noise about *Stockholm Syndrome*, and about arresting me."

Alex glanced at him then. "Is that one of your concerns and why you stay away?"

For a moment, Gabriel was speechless. "What? No. Evelyne isn't... Her feelings are genuine. I..." Gabriel could not remember a time he'd ever floundered in such a way, but the idea Evelyne might be *swayed* from a voluntary kidnapping...

"I know you took her at my behest, but you were her only contact," Alexandre continued, like this was a normal conversation. "Perhaps that is why you do not trust yourself, because you do not trust *her* feelings?"

"Evelyne is in love with me," Gabriel said firmly, temper snapping in every word. Until he reminded himself he didn't *want* her to be. "Which…is ridiculous, but I don't doubt that… Why are we talking about… I do not care what accusations the general throws at me," Gabriel insisted, not sure why he felt the need to defend Evelyne loving him when he wished she didn't. It wasn't the *point*. "General Vinyes is a fool. I simply wanted you to be aware he's skulking around making trouble. Not just with me. He made vague threats about *watching after Evelyne*."

For a moment, Alexandre studied him. When he spoke, it was with an odd carefulness Gabriel didn't recognize in his friend.

"So, he threw accusations at you, vaguely threatened that he'd be watching Evelyne, and you handled all of this without losing your temper, and instead came to me to address the situation. Is that correct?"

Gabriel blinked. It was correct, but… "I… I could have started a fight if I'd wanted to. I considered it." Not really, but a little bit. He'd *wanted* to hurt the general, but he knew…

"But you didn't. You didn't react with violence or anything over the top. You came to warn me. How odd. I thought violence was all you had in you when it came to those you loved?"

Gabriel could only stare at his friend. Speaking as though this had all been some…ridiculous setup.

"You…" Evidence. The only one who could have had evidence was… Alex. "This was a trap?"

Alexandre shrugged. "More or less."

"And if I'd fought him? If I'd created the scene that I'm very capable of creating?" Gabriel demanded.

"I would have sided with you," Alexandre returned, as though he'd thought it all out, but had already known what the outcome would be. "It might have even given me cause to dismiss the general, which would have been welcome indeed. But mostly I trusted you to make the right decision, Gabriel. Because you learned something all those years ago, whether you can accept that or not. You're not the same man you were. Because even then you were a *boy*."

Gabriel stood there, feeling a bit like he'd been stabbed through. Not the same man. But he was. How could he have changed?

Evelyne.

He shook away that thought. Perhaps some things had felt different, but that didn't make *it* different. His reaction to the general didn't make *him* different.

"I would like to think Evelyne and I could have made that clear to you," Alexandre continued. "Neither of us are fools, and neither of us find you to be a *monster*, but it turns out Ines was right. I had to show you."

Gabriel shook his head, trying to find some anchor amid all this crumbling inside him. If he listened to the crumbling, he'd have to believe he could...be what Evelyne and their child needed.

And he wanted that far too much to trust anything. "You tricked me. It shows...nothing."

Alexandre lifted a shoulder, reminding Gabriel a little too much of Evelyne. "Doesn't it?" Alex asked casually. "You didn't know it was a trick. You reacted. Handled it. Seems to show me quite a bit, honestly."

Gabriel was utterly speechless. He didn't have an argument. As much as he might have liked a scene, he had rationalized it out. Because he did not wish to hurt or complicate life for Alexandre or Evelyne, he had...resisted those urges inside him.

As though he could. As though he would, when it mattered. He had *done* it.

"She is miserable," Alexandre said, his voice quiet and serious. "She sits in the nursery and makes no decision. She ignores the staff trying to prod her into making decisions about the baby's name so we can begin the royal decrees necessary."

Gabriel rubbed at his heart, where an ache had not left him for some time but seemed to dive deeper now.

"And you are no better," Alexandre added.

"I have been working."

"You have been *hiding*. You have been *wallowing*. Why must you both insist on your own misery? You love one another."

Gabriel did not know what to do with this *word*. Love was for people who could handle such things.

Had he handled something? Could he... He shook his head. It all felt too dangerous, too...fragile. If he gave in, he'd spend the rest of his life walking the edge of violence.

Except General Vinyes had pushed all of his buttons and Gabriel had...handled it. Could it really mean what Alexandre wanted it to mean?

Gabriel eyed his friend, trying to understand where this had come from. Trying to find some old handle on his fear. "It is not like you to interfere."

Alexandre pulled a face. "No indeed. But here I am.

Take that as a sign things are dire indeed, and now it is up to *you* to fix it. You are rather good at fixing things."

He was. He *was*. He'd built a career out of fixing people's security problems for them in different ways.

But this was…

"You knew I would not make the wrong choice," Gabriel said, very carefully.

"Of course I knew, Gabriel," Alexandre said, very seriously. "I have been your friend our entire lives. I have also spent most of Evelyne's life doing what I could to protect her. I would not have allowed you anywhere near her if I thought that you also could not do the same. Just because you fell in love with her and got her pregnant under dubious circumstances doesn't mean you didn't protect her."

Gabriel sucked in a breath. There were few people he trusted as deeply as Alexandre, because Alex had always been there—and because he knew what exactly had happened with Gia. And Alex was right, there was no one he protected more fiercely than his sister.

"There are no protocol meetings to attend, are there?"

"Of course not. Go apologize to Evelyne. Make her happy. Or perhaps I will throw you in the dungeons after all…one of Evelyne's suggestions. Ines was a fan."

Gabriel chuckled in spite of himself. Yes, Evelyne would suggest that, but she wouldn't mean it. Because she loved him. She wanted him to be the man she thought he was. Not the monster he was so afraid of.

And if his best friend in the world could believe that of him, enough to set him up with the very real chance he might fight a *general*, Gabriel supposed he owed it to the both of them to decide to be the man they thought he was.

In every way possible.

"I will…see what I can do," Gabriel said a bit halt-ingly. He stepped forward, too many complicated emo-tions swamping him. "Thank you, for always being the brother I needed. Always."

Alexandre gave a sharp nod. "Likewise," he muttered, clearly uncomfortable. But meaning it.

Gabriel left the office, the anticipation he'd felt at see-ing Evelyne tenfold now that he wasn't going to fight it.

Alexandre was right about Evelyne's misery. Gabriel found her in the future nursery, surrounded by wallpa-per samples. Crying.

His heart cracked in two at the misery pouring out of her. Because of *him*. Because of his fears. His weaknesses.

He never wanted to watch her cry out of sorrow for him again. If there was any monster still inside him, he would remember Evelyne crying before he gave it any credence.

She looked up at him as he stepped into the room. Her expression showed no signs of surprise.

Or excitement. Or warmth. Just…resignation.

She wiped the tears away, made no move to excuse them or apologize for them. "I have been trying to decide between a zoo theme or an alphabet theme. It is quite a difficult choice."

She looked at the walls, clearly miserable. When she should feel joy and hope and excitement. All things she'd had before he'd inserted himself into her life.

Or all things she'd had until you ran away from it.

There could be no more of this. Not if it hurt her in such a way. It was no better than being a monster.

Gabriel cleared his throat, fighting past the tightness there. "I quite liked dogs when I was a young boy."

"Dogs," she repeated. She blinked. She looked around the room as if picturing it. "I have always wanted a dog."

"I imagine we could have one now." He used the *we* on purpose. And he let himself see it. Her. A baby. Their son. A dog running around. A family that he would protect, love, cherish.

Never run away from.

For a moment, she looked like she was considering it, then she shook her head and closed her eyes, more tears landing on her cheeks. "I wish you weren't here," she said, sounding a little petulant. "Go away."

But the words hurt even if he knew why she said them. He never wanted her to wish that again. "I… I'm sorry."

"You should be. You should be sorry about everything. Every damn thing."

This was his *principessa*. No cool looks, no detachment like those weeks ago when she'd *agreed* with him. And he could see it for what it was now. Fake. Trying to get through to him, trying to get him to realize his mistake.

Instead, he'd doubled down.

But he was here now, a new truth inside him. And she was being *herself.* Emotion and truth and just…*her*.

All those aches and pains and desperate cracks inside him that he'd been so sure were his due, were *necessary* in order to know he was doing the right thing, eased.

He moved closer to her, then crouched next to her. She eyed him with a scowl.

"What if I told you I was?" he asked. "Sorry. For all of it."

She looked up at him, tears on her cheeks he could not help but wipe away.

"I would not believe you," she said, but she didn't move away from his hands on her face.

"Why not?"

"Because I'm mad at you and I want to stay that way."

"Do you?"

Her lips trembled and she shook her head. "Why are you here?" she asked, her voice trembling.

"Alex…set me up. He put me in a volatile position, and when I did not react violently and obsessively, he pointed out that perhaps… I had learned something all those years ago. That actions have consequences, and I care about the result of mine."

She lifted her chin. Sniffed. "*I* tried to set you up and you stayed away. Why should I be impressed Alexandre got through to you?"

"Because you love me."

She said nothing to that, so he knew he needed more. All.

"I knew from the moment I danced with you at your eighteenth birthday ball that you would be a trouble to me. You were so vibrant and funny—even though I knew behind the scenes you were treated deplorably. I kept you at a distance from then on because there could never be surface. I felt that, even then."

She sniffed. "Well, I thought you were pompous and too skinny."

He grinned at her in spite of himself. "No, you didn't. You had a crush on me."

Her mouth twitched a little, though she did not smile. "Perhaps I thought you handsome, in spite of the pompous and the skinny. But I didn't hold a torch."

"No, you had the impressive Jordi."

She laughed, and he felt all those last worries melt away. Yes, he would do anything to protect her, protect *this*, the family they were creating, the love that existed between them. But that did not have to mean…

He was not a young man with too many emotions and not enough sense. He had grown into his sense, his control. He had learned, in part thanks to Alexandre, and in part thanks to life.

He could trust himself. He *had* to trust himself if he was to be a father.

And a good husband to the woman he loved.

"I love you, Evelyne. And I have been afraid to feel anything so deep as love, but it is undeniable, and I… I am not a boy. Perhaps you are right that I stopped maturing in that moment, but I would argue I *did* mature and learn and grow. I was just stuck thinking too little of myself because I was so ashamed of what I was capable of."

"And now you're not?"

"I am still ashamed, but I can accept that I have grown and learned. I can accept I am not the boy I was, even if some of his impulses live inside me. More, I want to accept those things, so that I can truly be your husband, and a father to our child. A good one, like mine was. Like you've always trusted me to be."

Evelyne had not prepared for this. She had a few fantasies—mostly where he begged on his hands and knees to come back and she sent him away, crushed and crying.

Then there were the ones where he swept in and demanded to be back in her life. They fought and argued like they had in Maine and ended up in her bed like then too.

She'd gotten some mileage out of both fantasies, but this was real life. And so this was more.

This was rational and adult and real. The things he'd learned or realized. The work he was willing to put in to…make this *love* work.

Love. He'd…said he loved her. Looked her right in the eye while he did. Like he was doing now, crouched next to her sitting on the floor. It could not be a comfortable position.

"What do you want, Evelyne?" he asked. "If it is for me to go away, I'm afraid I cannot abide it. But if it is all the things you said you wanted before, then I am here and ready to work for those things. Love and a life. I will work as hard as I can to earn this love you've given me. I will dive under every surface, fight any fear. For you." He put one hand over her stomach. "For him. And whoever else may come along."

Whoever else. Whatever tears she'd managed to fight back spilled forward again at the idea of more children. A real life. A real marriage. A real *future.*

"I love you, Gabriel. All I've ever wanted was for you to see yourself as I saw you. And admit you loved me back."

"I will still worry that I will…fall back into the boy who took things too far. That this love I have for you, for our son, is too much. Too big."

"Love is never too much," she told him, trying not to tremble apart. Trying to be strong, because they both needed it. They *all* needed it. "But should it be, you could trust me to pull you back."

"I could." He framed her face in his hands, held her gaze so directly and resolutely. "I do."

She was tired of crying, but she *did* have hormones to blame on some of it. "Don't leave again," she managed to croak.

"No. No, I won't." Then he was kissing her—the tears on her cheeks, her jaw. Her mouth. "I love you, Evelyne. You are mine and I am yours. Forever."

"Forever," she agreed.

EPILOGUE

THEIR SON WAS born on a stormy night in the palace. Evelyne said it reminded her of Maine, and that she pictured that balcony looking out over the ocean when the pain was too much.

Gabriel had never felt more helpless in his life. The nurse and midwife took him to task more than once for insisting they do more for his wife, but watching Evelyne suffer was his own suffering.

Until he heard his son cry. Then everything seemed to melt away. The nurse put a wriggling, mewling creature on his wife's chest, and their gazes met over his head. For a moment of pure, unadulterated bliss.

They were parents. They had a son.

When his son was placed into his arms, clean and bundled up, he knew there would be no running away in fear. No, from here on out, there could only be love, strength, support and doing whatever was required of him to be there for his son. Fight or acquiesce, support or lean, and always love.

Hours later, cleaned up and cuddled in together on the bed, the princess and her earl invited the king and queen to meet their nephew.

Alexandre and Ines entered together, but even in his

blissful state Gabriel noticed there was something...odd about them.

But they dutifully oohed and ahhed over the baby—from opposite sides of the bed. Alexandre expressed some frustration over the fact there was still no name to go out on the royal decree, but Evelyne only told him to be patient.

When they left at the nurse's insistence that Evelyne needed her rest, it was without ever once having looked at one another.

"They're awfully icy with one another," Evelyne murmured, her head on Gabriel's shoulder, her gaze on their baby.

"I believe they had a bit of a row earlier," Gabriel murmured, stroking the babe's cheek.

"But Alexandre and Ines never fight," Evelyne said, lifting her gaze—briefly—to Gabriel. Then back to their son, like she couldn't bear to look away for more than a minute any more than Gabriel could.

"I heard shouting this morning," he told her. "And Alexandre was very distracted during our morning meeting."

"Hmm." But the troubles of Alexandre and Ines had nothing on the beautiful, sleeping boy in her arms. They both watched him in fully content silence.

"He is perfect," Evelyne said after a while.

Gabriel would have to insist she sleep soon, but he couldn't quite bring himself to take the baby away from her. Not just yet.

"He is at that. We have to name him, Evelyne. No more putting it off."

She pouted. "It's just so permanent. What if we pick the wrong name?"

"No name is wrong. Because he is perfect regardless."

"I guess this is true." She tucked the blanket under his chin, stroked a finger down his cheek. Then she looked up at Gabriel. "Do you remember back in Maine when I said I would not be naming him after you?"

"Vividly, *principessa*." He kissed her temple, and she leaned into him even more.

"Perhaps that is our answer. Let us give him the names of all the good men in our lives. Your father. Alexandre. *You*, who saved me."

While he still struggled to consider himself a *good* man, Gabriel liked the idea, because it would be a constant reminder of what he *should* be.

So their child was christened Gabriel Manuel Alexandre Marti, and both his parents knew he would someday make Alis a most wonderful king.

But more importantly, he would be a good man, surrounded by love. Always.

* * * * *

Did Secretly Pregnant Princess *sweep you off your feet? Then you're sure to enjoy the next installment in the Babies for Royal Brides duet, coming soon! And why not explore these other stories by Lorraine Hall?*

Princess Bride Swap
The Bride Wore Revenge
A Wedding Between Enemies
Pregnant, Stolen, Wed
Unwrapping His Forbidden Assistant

Available now!

Get up to 4 Free Books!

**We'll send you 2 free books from each series you try
PLUS a free Mystery Gift.**

FREE Value Over $25

Both the **Harlequin Presents** and **Harlequin Medical Romance** series
feature exciting stories of passion and drama.

YES! Please send me 2 FREE novels from Harlequin Presents or Harlequin Medical Romance and my FREE gift (gift is worth about $10 retail). After receiving them, if I don't wish to receive any more books, I can return the shipping statement marked "cancel." If I don't cancel, I will receive 6 brand-new larger-print novels every month and be billed just $7.19 each in the U.S., or $7.99 each in Canada, or 4 brand-new Harlequin Medical Romance Larger-Print books every month and be billed just $7.19 each in the U.S. or $7.99 each in Canada, a savings of 20% off the cover price. It's quite a bargain! Shipping and handling is just 50¢ per book in the U.S. and $1.25 per book in Canada.* I understand that accepting the 2 free books and gift places me under no obligation to buy anything. I can always return a shipment and cancel at any time. The free books and gift are mine to keep no matter what I decide.

Choose one:
- ☐ **Harlequin Presents Larger-Print** (176/376 BPA G36Y)
- ☐ **Harlequin Medical Romance** (171/371 BPA G36Y)
- ☐ **Or Try Both!** (176/376 & 171/371 BPA G36Z)

Name (please print)

Address   Apt. #

City   State/Province   Zip/Postal Code

Email: Please check this box ☐ if you would like to receive newsletters and promotional emails from Harlequin Enterprises ULC and its affiliates. You can unsubscribe anytime.

Mail to the **Harlequin Reader Service:**
IN U.S.A.: P.O. Box 1341, Buffalo, NY 14240-8531
IN CANADA: P.O. Box 603, Fort Erie, Ontario L2A 5X3

Want to explore our other series or interested in ebooks? Visit www.ReaderService.com or call 1-800-873-8635.